Visit us at www.boldstrokesbooks.com

STRAIGHT BOY ROOMMATE

STRAIGHT BOY ROOMMATE

by

Kev Troughton

2013

STRAIGHT BOY ROOMMATE

© 2013 By Kev Troughton. All Rights Reserved.

ISBN 10: 1-60282-782-6
ISBN 13: 978-1-60282-782-0

This Trade Paperback Original Is Published By
Bold Strokes Books, Inc.
P.O. Box 249
Valley Falls, NY 12185

First Edition: January 2013

Credits
Editor: Cindy Cresap
Production Design: Susan Ramundo
Cover Design By Sheri (graphicartist2020@hotmail.com)

CHAPTER ONE

It's Friday afternoon and I'm panicking. Today's the last day for new students to register, so today I'm going to find out who I'm sharing my room with.

I'd let my parents talk me into getting a shared room. "It'll be much cheaper," they'd said, and as they're paying, I couldn't argue. They had other reasons, too, lots of stuff about not getting lonely, making new friends, and sharing things. They said it would be nice. I said okay.

I knew from the start that it wouldn't be nice. I knew it would be shit. The only question was just how shit. I'd thought through all sorts of scenarios, ranging from the best (a bit shit), to the worst (so shit I have to leave uni before Christmas).

I'd made a list of all the reasons why I didn't want a shared room. Just a mental list, obviously. I hadn't written it down, that would have been sad.

Reasons why a shared room is a shit idea:

1. I need to wank all the time.
2. Even though I'm 18, my cock still has a mind of its own, and I can't stop it getting hard at random times.
3. I bought a Fleshlight for my 18th birthday, and I want to use it all the time.

4. I need to watch loads of porn (being honest, I suppose this should be "I *want* to watch loads of porn").
5. My roommate will be a twat.
6. My roommate will be a geek.
7. My roommate will be an unbearable, arrogant bastard.
8. My roommate will be super hot and I'll get a boner and drool over him, and he'll notice, and then I'm fucked.
9. My roommate won't be hot at all, and I'll hate him for not being hot.
10. I really do need to wank all the time.

How many of these did I share with my parents? Guess.

I've had four wanks already, and I only got here yesterday afternoon. The best one was this morning, sitting in front of my computer, watching amazing porn, and fucking my Fleshlight. And any time now, some fucking nobhead roommate is going to arrive and that will be the end of all that.

Besides, I'd decided that going away to uni was going to be my chance to come out. I mean, a few people (two girls) back home know I'm gay, but they're sworn to secrecy. This was going to be the time I came out properly, but sharing a room fucks that up too. I've tried the conversation out in my head so many times. After, "Hi, I hope you don't mind sharing your bedroom with a homosexual," it all goes wrong.

I think I should go back down to the student union where they're allocating the rooms. I might ask someone if they've got a list. Find out his name, at least, and check he's still coming. Perhaps he won't turn up. There's always a few people who don't turn up, aren't there?

I grab a hoodie and pull it on as I head for the door. A quick look round to make sure my computer's off and I've not left anything dodgy lying around, and then out and down the stairs.

The SU's busy, people meeting up, heading for the bars and cafes, signing up for things. The big room at the back isn't as full as yesterday when I arrived. Four tables with student volunteers behind them, a short queue in front of each table. One of the volunteers is quite a good-looking guy in skinny jeans, and I head toward his queue. But then I spot an even better looking guy, in the queue next to the one I've joined.

Two seconds later, I'm standing behind him, from where I can safely check him out. He's a bit taller than me, nice muscly body, in a T-shirt that shows off quite broad shoulders and a slim waist. Very nice. Skate trainers too. I've got a bit of a thing about guys in trainers. I'm wondering if he actually skates, or if he's just into the skater boy look. I'm wondering what size trainers he takes, and if they'd fit me. I'm having a good look at his arse, too, where there's quite a lot of his tight boxers showing over his belt. Fucking hot. I'm getting hard already. I'm in my baggy jeans, so getting a boner isn't a problem. I love getting hard near to guys I'm perving over, maybe risking a bit of a feel in my pocket.

He's at the front of his queue now, and leaning over the table, which gives me an even better chance to check out the shape of his arse in his jeans. I can't hear what he's saying at first, but it seems to be getting louder, then it's up to shouting level. He's swearing a lot, and the girl at the table's saying there's nothing she can do. I can't quite get what the problem is, so I move in closer, right up behind him, close enough to get a whiff of his aftershave.

Suddenly, it's all over. He bangs the table with his hand, shouts, "Fuck it, then!" and turns sharply round to storm out. But I'm too close behind him, and he knocks into me, sending me sprawling backward over someone's sports bag that they've put on the floor behind me.

I go down like a stone and hit the back of my head on the floor. I think I hit it quite hard. It hurts like fuck anyway. A few people react and start to crowd round as I sit up, trying to hold my head and rub it at the same time. I don't really hear what anyone's saying for a few seconds. My head's a bit fuzzy, and then skater guy squats down in front of me and starts apologizing and asking if I'm okay. I don't reply straightaway, and he puts his hand on my shoulder and asks again.

I start to tell everyone I'm fine. "I'm just a bit shaken up, okay? Give me a minute, yeah?" I'm happy staying here for a bit. The view's fantastic. Skater boy's squatting down on his heels right in front of me, with his knees way apart and his crotch virtually in my face. I notice he's still wearing his wristbands from the summer music festivals, the same ones I went to, by the look of it. Then I notice his T-shirt, which has "Masturbating is not a Crime" printed across the front, just the shirt I almost bought a few months ago, but bottled out as usual.

He holds his hand out for me to take hold of, to help me up. As I take it, I wonder if it's the one he uses for wanking; I hope it is. He's looking hard at me. "How's your head, mate? Do you want to sit down somewhere?"

"Maybe I'll sit outside for a bit; get some air." I'm hoping he'll come with me, and he does. There's a railing just outside, and I lean on it. My head still hurts like fuck, but the dizziness is going. "I'll be all right. Don't worry."

"Look, mate, I feel really bad about this. Can I get you a beer or something?"

"No, it's fine, really."

"How about some of this?" His hand disappears into the pocket of his jeans, and I wonder for a second where this is going, then his hand reappears with a small bag of weed in it. "What do you think?"

"Yeah, that'd be good. Might even take the pain away a bit."

He's looking round for the best direction to walk, and then we set off over the road and across the grass. We make some small talk about Glastonbury and Leeds; the bands we saw, the best sets, the atmosphere, the girl who fell into the toilet. I do a good impression of being as relaxed and casual as he is, but walking so close to this really hot guy means I'm about as relaxed as a coiled spring.

We soon get to a set of steps leading down to some old huts. Maybe they're used by gardeners or something. Anyway, they're completely deserted at the moment, and it seems like a safe place to have a smoke. The steps have a low wall running down each side of them, and he sits on the bottom step with his back against the wall. I sit opposite him with my back against the wall on the other side, facing directly toward him. As he rolls the joint, I've got the perfect view, and I start getting hard again.

I need to start a conversation; you know, be relaxed and natural. "Your T-shirt's mint. I was going to buy one, but I didn't in the end."

"Oh, mate, you should have. People's reactions are fucking classic. Why didn't you get one?"

"I'm a big, fucking pussy, and I bottled out." I smile, and he grins back at me and then lights the joint.

We share it in silence for a while, and then he looks across at me. "How's your head?"

"It's okay. This is helping." I gesture at the joint. "What was going on back there, anyway? I heard some of it, but I couldn't really."

"It's a fucking nightmare, I tell you. I got here last night, and I'm in a room with the geek from hell. He's a complete twat."

I think about my anti-room-sharing list. "I'm sharing too. Mine hasn't arrived yet. He'll probably be just as bad."

"Doubt it. Mine would win twat of the year, seriously. Twat of the century. He wound me up so much last night I ended up yelling at him and storming out."

"What, you've had a row with him already?"

"Yeah. I put up with him for about an hour, but I'd had enough after about five minutes."

"Perhaps he was just having a bad day."

"And perhaps he's just a cunt. He looked at me like he thought I was a piece of shit and then started complaining about everything. 'You're not going to try and smoke in the room, are you?' 'I think it's best if we don't play music when the other one is in, because I suspect our taste in music will be wildly different, and yours will probably annoy me.' 'I hope you're not going to leave all your things lying around, because untidiness makes me tense.' Seriously, mate, I wanted to smack him. Anyway, in the end, I thought, if he's going to be a cunt, I will be too. So I told him the main reason I'd come to uni was to have as much sex as possible, so when I brought a girl back for a shag, he'd have to fuck off somewhere else, and if he ever managed to find anyone to have sex with, I'd do the same. He didn't seem to like that very much."

"I'm not surprised."

"So then he got really bitchy. 'That's just the level I might have expected from someone who needs to wear a shirt with a puerile slogan like that on it.' That kind of thing. I was really fucking mad by now, so I told him I usually have about four wanks a day, but my record is nine, and he'll have to fuck off somewhere every time I need a wank too, and that I watch porn all the time on my computer, and if guys with big dicks fucking hot chicks makes him feel inadequate, that's tough fucking shit, and he should get a fucking life."

"Jesus. What did he say then?" This isn't the question I really want to ask. What I really want to know is whether the four wanks a day thing is true or not, but I don't dare ask him, even after half a spliff.

"He didn't say anything. He just turned his back on me and started unpacking stuff out of one of his boxes. After a bit, I started feeling a twat, just standing there, so I went out and slammed the door."

"Have you been back?"

"Had to in the end. I got fucking wasted in the bar, then went back about twelve. He was just lying there, facing toward the wall, but I don't think he was asleep. So I got into bed and had the loudest wank in the history of the world. I wanted to get a reaction off him, but he didn't move or say anything."

"What about this morning?"

"I was pretty hung over. By the time I woke up, he'd gone."

I'm not sure what to think about all this. Maybe he's a really great, confident guy who doesn't take any shit off people, or maybe he's a selfish, arrogant fucker and on a big ego trip. I know which way I'm going to play it though. "I think you're a fucking legend, mate. I always imagine saying that kind of stuff to people, but I never do."

"It felt good at the time, but I'm pretty fucked now, though, aren't I?"

"So is that why you were arguing with that girl back in there? Were you trying to get a different room?"

"Yeah."

"Won't they do it?"

"No."

"Shit." I look over at him again. He's getting the bag of weed out of his pocket again. Then he stretches his legs out in front of him and crosses them at the ankles. His trainers are just a couple of inches from my hand now, and I start to imagine my hand moving across slowly, sliding up the leather, my fingers moving inside, feeling the warm sweatiness inside his shoe, feeling the shape of his foot inside his sock, then moving up further, inside the leg of his jeans, rubbing up against the hair on his leg. Fucking hell. My cock gets even harder, gives a bit of a jolt, and I feel some pre-cum dribbling out.

If I let that fantasy go on much longer, I'm going to cum in my pants. With an effort, I try to get the conversation restarted instead. "So if they won't change any of the rooms, I hope they haven't put me with some dickhead."

"You'll be all right. You seem pretty chilled. You'll get on with more or less anyone."

"I suppose. I know what'll happen though. I'll just fit in with whatever he wants, like I always do. I'll end up getting walked over."

"Bollocks. You just have to make it clear from the start, you know, how you want to do things."

"But I'm crap at that."

"What do you mean?"

"Being, you know, assertive with people. I never know what to say or how to say it. Not at the time, anyway. I suddenly think of what I should have said after the conversation's over."

"You've got to decide before then. Plan it out. Make a list of things you want to say."

I laugh and he looks up from the spliff. "What?"

I decide to be honest with him. I don't think I need to hide things from a guy in a "Masturbating is not a Crime" T-shirt. "I have got a sort of list, actually. When I found out I was going to have to share, I made a list of all the reasons why I didn't want to."

He's stopped rolling now and is looking at me and trying to read my expression. I wonder what he sees. It must interest him because he continues, "Come on, then, mate. What's on your list?" He sees me hesitate. "It can't be as bad as mine."

"Was your list all the stuff you said to your roommate about…er…"

"Sex and wanking? Yeah, mostly." He gives me a really hot grin.

"Well, mine's about the same as yours then, really. Except not the one about getting laid all the time. I'm not expecting too much on that score. The others though. The wanking one. And the porn on the computer."

"Cool." Just that. Then he looks down again and finishes the spliff. I'm looking at his legs again, and I hear the lighter click and his breath as he sucks in a huge lungful. As he breathes out, the question comes with it. "So why don't we share?"

"What? But we can't. You said they won't let you change rooms."

"We don't have to tell anyone. We'll just do it. By the time anyone finds out, it'll be easier to just let us carry on. We'll say we made a mistake with the room numbers."

"What about when the guy arrives who's supposed to be in my room?"

"We'll tell him it got changed and send him to my room."

"But, what if—"

"Hey, I thought you might like the idea. We don't have to."

"It isn't that. It's just…"

"If you were sharing with me, you could do what the fuck you wanted. You want to watch porn, you tell me to fuck off for an hour, no problem. Or you just do it while I'm in the room. I really don't give a shit. If you want to jack off any time I'm there, it won't be a problem for me. I don't get embarrassed about guys wanking. I played rugby right through school, yeah? And I shared a room with my older brother for years. He was a proper dirty cunt."

"It sounds okay." *Okay?* What am I saying? It sounds fucking amazing.

"Shall we go for it then?"

"Yeah, I suppose."

"Great. Have some of this, then we can go and move my stuff." He holds out the spliff, and I take it. A million images crowd into my head at once, getting dirtier and dirtier, more and more exciting. Him getting undressed in front of me. Him wanking in front of his computer, with me standing behind him. Him fucking a girl while I watch. Me kneeling in front of him and sucking him off.

Then reality hits. "Look, I don't think it's a good idea."

He's genuinely taken aback. "Why the fuck not?"

Deep breath. "I'm gay."

"Good one. Come on, what's the real problem?"

"No, seriously. I'm gay."

"Bollocks!"

"Okay then. If *you* say I'm not gay, I suppose I can't be."

"Come on, mate, don't dick around."

"I'm not dicking around. I'm serious. I can't share a room with you because I'm gay, and it would just be…impossible."

"Fucking hell, you really mean this, don't you? I never would have guessed though. How long have you been gay for?" Even really hot guys can ask fucking stupid questions.

"How long have you been straight for?"

"What? I've always…Oh, I see…yeah. Sorry, mate, I just wasn't expecting…Fuck." I take another huge drag on the spliff and put it out on the step. But he's not finished yet.

"And you're seriously gay? I mean, like full-on? Not just a bit AC/DC?"

"Do you want me to prove it to you or something?" As soon as I say it, I wish I hadn't, but his smile seems to mean I've got away with it.

"No, mate. You're all right. I don't swing that way, okay?" Then a new thought. "Sharing with a queer, though, a gay, I mean, it could be a right laugh. You could give me advice about what to wear. It'd be like that program on the telly."

"Look. I don't think you've quite got it." He looks blank, and I realize I've got no alternative but to plow on. "Think about it. What happens the first time you need to get undressed? You'll be wondering what I'm thinking. I'll be trying not to look at you. It'll just be awkward all the time."

"Well, it doesn't have to be."

"It'll be a fucking nightmare. Look. What if I need a wank in bed tonight? You say I'd be able to just jack off whenever I wanted, but it wouldn't work, would it? You'd be wondering if I'm wanking over you or not, and I'd know you were wondering—"

"Wow, fucking hell. Would you be? I mean, if...*would* you be wanking over me?"

Shit! Why did he have to ask that? Why did I have to use that example? It makes it so obvious I fancy him? Oh well, fuck it. Like they say, I've started so I'll finish.

"Probably. No. More than probably."

"So you? Shit. Would you seriously want to wank over me?" He seems amazed that a guy could possibly fancy him. It obviously hasn't entered his head that if he's fanciable for girls, he's fanciable for gay guys as well. I manage a small nod. "How hot do you think I am, then? Come on, out of ten."

"For fuck's sake. I'm not answering that."

"That means a ten. Result!"

"No, not ten. Nowhere near ten. Seriously." I look over at him, and he's got a massive fuck off grin right across his face.

He's irresistible. "Really, I mean, no more than a nine and a half."

He studies my face carefully, and his grin fades a bit. "Sorry. I suppose I shouldn't have asked you that. It was a bit out of order."

"Would you ask a girl that kind of question?"

"Yeah, I probably would, mate." I believe he really would. Probably he has.

"Well, I suppose it's all right, then. Fuck. You're a head case."

"Nine and a half? Really?" I nod. I can't stop myself. "Hey, cheers for telling me, mate. I mean, you could have lied."

"I didn't want to. I don't want to start in on something that isn't...fair. Just think about it. It'd be like you having to share a room with a really hot girl. She's super hot, and you fancy the arse off her, but she's not interested in you at all. Perhaps...perhaps she's a lesbian, or something. She's just there all the time, getting naked, and being hot, and not letting you do anything. It'd be a nightmare."

"But what if..." He pauses as he thinks it through. "What if she said she didn't mind? What if she said it was all cool? Like, I could perv over her as much as I liked, and wank myself stupid over her, and she...she'd, you know, think it was a bit of a turn-on, having someone who, you know..." He's kind of running out of words now, but he's said enough for me to get the point.

"Are you saying...Are you saying you'd actually like it if I was..."

"Yeah, why not? I think it'd turn me on a bit. I don't mean you'd turn me on. I mean, knowing you're fucking watching me, and getting off on it, and I can, you know, get you going really easily." He starts to rub his hands over his body, in porn star style. He rubs over his chest, and puts one hand inside his

T-shirt and over his nipple. It's the first view I've had of his body, and it's muscly and hot. He only gives me a second or two though, then he moves both hands down to his crotch and starts rubbing his thighs and round his bollocks. Fuck, he's right about getting me going easily. "Liking that?"

I don't answer. I figure the answer's obvious.

"Better stop that before you cum in your pants. Fuck. Your face was classic."

I try to look like someone who isn't rock hard and drooling. "I really don't know what you mean."

"Look. Are we going to do this thing or not? I'm up for it. I think it'd be a fucking massive laugh. And kind of a bit dangerous too, you know? Exciting. Come on, what do you think? Be honest."

"Well, to be honest, I can't really believe this is happening, and I expect it'll all fuck up in about ten minutes, but it's just about the most exciting thing that's ever happened to me, and…shit, I don't know what to say."

"That's sorted then. One thing though. Just so we know where we are with this. I'm proper, full-on straight, yeah? I'm not one of those metrosexuals or whatever they call it. I'm just not interested in lads, not that way. So no touching, okay? I don't want to wake up and find you feeling me up or something. You all right with that?"

"Yeah. That's cool." I've no idea whether it's cool or not. I don't know how this is going to turn out. Still, even if it does fuck up, it'll be a fucking exciting fuck up.

"Right. Shall we go and rescue my shit before that cunt throws it into the corridor?"

He starts to get up, but I'm so hard it's almost hurting. I know I've got to tell him, got to start this the way I mean to go on. "Um. Look. There is one thing…before we…I need a wank."

He laughs, loud and uninhibited. "What, now?"

"Yes, now. I'm fucking desperate, actually."

"Come on, then. Let's go and find the nearest bogs so you can do the business." Before I know quite what's happening, we're up and walking back to the student union building. He's so relaxed about the whole thing that I'm hardly embarrassed at all. I don't think I've ever said anything like that to anyone before. I would have expected to be bright red and cringing, but actually, I'm fine. I'm walking next to my new, hot, straight mate, so we can find a toilet and I can have a wank. Over him. And he's cool with it. I look across at him as we walk and he's still smiling. Then he puts an arm over my shoulder and leans in. "So have you got a boner?"

"Yes."

"And is it because of me?"

"What do you think? Of course it's because of you."

"How long you had a boner then?"

"Since just before you knocked me over in there." We're nearly back at the SU and I gesture across to the building.

"What? Were you already perving over me then? Shit! I thought you were standing a bit close, but fucking hell. You've been hard all this time? I think that probably puts you in my top five dirtiest motherfuckers I've ever met." He stops to think for a moment. "Actually no, probably not the top five, but you're definitely the dirtiest homo I've ever met."

"Out of how many?" He laughs and pushes open the door to the SU. The toilets are just opposite the entrance and we go inside. I'm not sure how this is going to work, but I walk into the nearest cubicle, and he doesn't follow, so I shut and lock the door.

I hear him go into the next cubicle along and then the noise of the seat being dropped down. I don't think he's shut the door, though. "Come on, then, tiger. Fucking give it hell."

I fumble with my belt and manage to get it undone. My hands are shaking so much I can hardly get my jeans down. I can hear the blood pounding in my ears, and my cock is twitching and throbbing inside my boxers. I grab the waistband and push them down. My cock's so hard it actually hurts. I sit on the seat and take a few deep breaths. Then his voice comes through the partition again. "How long you going to need? You're not going to be in there ages are you?"

"About a minute, probably."

"Fuck. You always cum that fast?"

"Only when there's a fucking hot guy sitting right next to me."

"And when he knows exactly what you're doing, right?"

"Yeah, that helps." I grab hold of my dick and move my hand up the shaft. A big sticky drop of pre-cum oozes out, and I rub it into my bell-end and start some serious, slow wanking. Never mind a minute, I could cum in about five seconds. I'm not going to rush this. I want to make it last at least a bit. On the other side of the partition, I hear him shifting his weight, and now I can see one of his feet under the partition.

"How's it feeling in there, mate? You having a good time?"

"Fucking amazing." Seeing his foot in the small gap below the partition gives me a sudden surge of lust. "Hey. Move your foot a bit."

"What? Oh, okay." He moves it away from the partition, where I can't see it anymore!

"Not that way, you twat. Toward me. Move it closer to me."

"You got some weird fetish thing? Foot fetish or something?" But he moves his foot back anyway, right up to the partition.

"Yeah. Feet, trainers, socks, the whole lot."

"Dirty fucker. I suppose this must be like all your birthdays coming at the same time, then." His other foot appears for a moment and pushes his trainer off. He flexes his toes for a bit and then pushes the discarded trainer under the partition into my cubicle. His foot, in its white sports sock, is on my side of the partition now, and he's moving it about, like he's showing it off to me. I resist the temptation to pick up his trainer and sniff it. Instead, I take off my own trainer and slip my foot into his. The warm sweatiness inside and the unfamiliar shape that his foot has molded it into drive me straight to the edge. I'm going to cum. I start really pumping my dick, and I realize I'm getting very noisy, but it's too late to worry about that. The first shot of cum hits the partition, followed by another and another. It's going everywhere, and I'm loving it. It's the most intense orgasm I've had for ages, and it just seems to go on and on.

I'm still coming down from it and starting to get my breath back when his voice comes through the partition again, "Mate? You cum already? You were proper horned up, weren't you? Can I have my trainer back now, you perv?"

I look down and there's cum everywhere. Most of it's on the partition and the floor, but there's quite a lot on my boxers and jeans, which are down round my ankles, and quite a lot on his trainer too. Now his voice comes from in front of me, he's moved round to stand outside the door to my cubicle. "Come on, what the fuck are you doing to it, fetish boy?"

"I'm not doing anything to it. Well, I'm wearing it. I hope you don't mind. You did push it underneath."

"Do I get it back then?"

"Yeah, sorry. Look, I've got a bit of, well, I've cum on it a bit." There's a pause, and I'm not sure how he's going to react.

I wait…then, "Well you better keep it, then. I'm not touching it if you've jizzed all over it. Here—" Suddenly, his other trainer is being pushed under the door. "Give me yours."

"Hang on." I rush to get my jeans done up. My boxers feel wet between my legs, but what the fuck? I open the door, and he's standing outside, looking even more sexy than I remembered. I pick my trainers up and hand them to him. He studies them in mock seriousness, looking for any telltale white stains. Then he drops them onto the floor and slips his feet into them. While I put his other trainer on and sort out my belt, he's surveying the ribbons of shining white cum on the partition and the floor. He shakes his head, but the smile is still there.

"Disgusting. Absolutely fucking disgusting. And I suppose you're just going to leave all this shit, are you?"

"Yeah. I thought I might."

"You should be fucking ashamed."

"I am. I really am."

"You don't fucking look it." Big grins from both of us. "Right, let's go and sort our room out. If you're a good boy, we can have some porn on later, and then I'll show you what a proper cum-shot looks like."

Chapter Two

O h. I'm Dan by the way. It's weird; I know the dodgiest stuff about you, but I don't know what your name is."

"And I don't know *anything* about you. I'm Tom. I know it's a really boring name. Half the boys in my school were called Tom. So don't take the piss."

"Could be worse. You could be called Dick. I'll see if I can think of something better to call you. You'll have to give me a while, though."

"What? You mean, like a nickname? That'd be cool. Nothing rude though."

"Rude? Me?"

For the second time in an hour, we're heading out of the SU building together, but this time, we don't go down across the grass, we turn left and follow the road round to where his accommodation block is.

I'm still wearing his trainers, which is a big turn-on, and I'm walking next to my new, straight, dirty-as-fuck mate, soon to be roommate, which has me so turned on I can hardly control myself! My hard-on hasn't gone down at all since I spunked up in the SU bogs, and I can feel it rubbing nicely against the inside of my jeans, through the thin material of my boxers. I look down at his left trainer as I walk; the splashes of cum are still there, on the toe and the laces, starting to dry by now, I suppose.

We get to the front door of the block, and he has his key ready to let us in. He takes the stairs two at a time, and I follow him. We turn along the second floor corridor, and he looks back over his shoulder toward me. "Now, I'm not going to be rude to him, okay. We're just going to go in, fetch my stuff, and come out." I don't know if he's trying to convince me or himself.

He puts his key in the door and opens it. Facing us is the most boring eighteen-year-old in the whole of England. The most interesting thing you could say about him is that he's quite tall. Boring hair: brownish and smartish. Boring clothes: a plain shirt, tucked in. Old-fashioned jeans with a crease ironed in neatly, and shiny brown shoes. For fuck's sake.

He's sitting at his computer, and as we come in he looks up for a second, gives an obvious, rather theatrical sigh, and goes back to his screen. I look across at Dan and can see him tense up. He's going to start on the guy. I can see it coming. I try to mouth "Ignore him" but it's too late. "So, cunt face. What's the big fucking sigh supposed to mean? I thought you'd be fucking pleased to see us." So much for not being rude, but the guy deserves it; he's being a proper douche bag.

We wait for a reply. He doesn't even look up, but I can see how uptight he is. Dan wanders over a bit closer.

"Now, I can understand how you don't want to be nice to me, on account of you thinking I'm a disgusting, dirty motherfucker, but you haven't said hi to my sweet, innocent friend, either, and he's starting to think you might be a bit fucking rude."

This time, bland-boy looks up for all of two seconds, says "Hi," through gritted teeth, and then makes a big show of going back to his typing.

Dan's just getting warmed up, though. "So did we catch you at a bad time?" He turns to me, his face a picture of studied seriousness. "I think he was just about to have a wank over Luke Skywalker or something, and we've disturbed him. Maybe he was just going to get his light saber out." He gestures with his eyes across to the wall next to bland-boy's bed, and yes, there is a *Star Wars* poster. I crack up; I don't mean to, but I can't stop myself.

But the *Star Wars* insult obviously hits a raw nerve. Perhaps he really does wank over Luke Skywalker. His mouth opens and closes a couple of times, as if he can't quite decide which carefully phrased put-down to use, then he gets up, storms toward the door, and wrenches it open. On the way out, he stops long enough to shout, "Piss off. Both of you!" and then he's gone.

Dan looks quite taken aback. "Well, that was nice."

"It might make things easier, though. At least we don't have to make small talk."

"True. Right. Let's get started. I haven't unpacked anything really, so it won't take long." We move round quickly, him collecting up his toothbrush and toiletries, me putting a few things into boxes, and then he looks around the room. "Well, I think that's it." He opens a couple of random drawers, and then throws the duvet off the bed. "No, nothing there. Except a few spunky stains. Wanna look?"

"No. Of course not." But I can't stop myself going over and looking. Although the cum's completely dry, it's yellow enough to show clearly against the white sheet. There's a lot of it. I get a sudden mental picture of Dan lying on that sheet, on his side, his hand pumping his nob and his body tensing and jerking as he shoots his load. A serious amount of pre-cum leaks into my boxers, and I think I make a little noise, because Dan looks over at me. "Wanna lick?"

Oh God, I'd love to! I can't tell him that, though. "Fuck off. I'm not a pervert."

He explodes with laughter and then slaps his hand to his forehead. "Der, no, of course you're not. I must have mixed you up with some other fucking homo sleazebag."

I grin and give him the finger. "Right. Sweet and innocent, like you said."

I drag myself away from the bed and pick up a couple of bags. I would have been quite happy having a bit longer to look at those cum splashes, and maybe even…no, for fuck's sake, what's wrong with me?

But Dan isn't picking bags up, he gone across to geek boy's computer. "Hey, Tom, he's left this on, mate." As I go across, he's already sitting down and clicking the mouse.

"Dan, what you doing? Looking for porn?"

"No. He won't have any. Well, not yet, anyway."

"Oh, you're not…Shit. He'll go mad when he finds it."

"Let's hope so." I go round behind the desk and join Dan at the keyboard. He's already on a porn website, one of his favorites, I suppose, and I watch as he starts to copy and paste pictures into various folders in geek boy's My Documents. Then he's on the guy's Facebook. James Smith—even his name's dull. Dan types in a new status: "James Smith has found out, since arriving at uni, that he likes sucking big penises." It only takes a few minutes. "Right, Tom. Your turn."

We swap seats, and I bring up a website that I know has plenty of suitable pics. As I'm clicking on a picture of a hot guy in a cowboy hat sitting on a massive cock, I realize, fleetingly, that it's the first time I've let anyone see any of the porn that I've been watching almost every day for the last four or five years. Dan doesn't seem bothered, though, then he stabs his finger at the screen. "That one." The picture is of a skinny guy with blond hair getting spit roasted. "Make that one his screensaver." I set about it, and it's soon done.

"Right then. Let's get going."

We're just picking up the bags and boxes when a glance at the bed sets me thinking about Dan's spunk again. Before I can change my mind, I blurt out, "Hang on a minute. Before we go, there's just something I've got to do."

Dan watches me as I go over and sit on the bed. Watches as I put my hand out and trace the pattern of the cum with my finger.

"You're not really going to?"

"It was your idea."

"Was it fuck. How was it my idea?"

"You said, 'Did I want a lick?' Well, I do."

"I didn't think you'd actually fucking do it."

"Teach you to be more careful what you say in future, then."

I grab a handful of the sheet and pull it so it comes untucked. I lift it up toward my face, and look for the bit with the biggest stain on it. Dan comes and sits opposite me on the bed. "I can't believe you're doing this."

"Do you want me to stop? Am I being too pervy for you?"

"No. Be as pervy as you like."

"How many loads is this?"

"What?"

"How many loads? Is this just last night, or did you have another one this morning?"

"Mate. I had two this morning. Only one of them's here, though. The other one was in the shower."

I push a big piece of the sheet into my mouth, and start to wet it with my spit. I can feel the material soften as I move it round my mouth, and the taste of the cum is soon there. It's very faint, but definitely there, salty and sharp on my tongue.

My cock is so hard, I think I might cum in my pants, and I lean back on the bed, so I can get my hand down the front of my jeans. Dan reaches out and grabs hold of my wrist. "Not yet! You can do that in a bit. We need to get out before that cunt gets back."

I let the wet sheet drop out of my mouth. "Shit. I'd forgotten about him."

"Get your hand out of your pants, then. Fucking hell, can't you leave it alone for two minutes?"

"Okay, okay. We'll go." Reluctantly, I get up off the bed and pick up the bags.

This time we do make it out the door. There's too much stuff for one journey, so we carry the first load to where it's still in view, put it down, and then go back for the second. Eventually, we get everything out of his block and into mine, or ours, as it will be now. We stop for a rest at the bottom of the stairs. Dan's looking across at me and grinning. "You licked my dried up spunk on a bedsheet. What kind of dirty fucker does that make you?"

I grin back. "You suggested I should lick your spunk off a bedsheet. What does that make you?" Dan seems to be considering the question carefully, but he obviously can't decide on the answer, because he just shrugs, smiles, and picks up the bags again.

After a couple more minutes, we've managed to get everything along the corridor and piled outside the door, and then I search through my pockets until I find the key.

When I open the door to my room, there's someone in there.

My roommate has arrived, and he's unpacking stuff into the wardrobe. As soon as we come in, he stops what he's doing and comes over to us. "Hey, I'm Ryan. Looks like we're sharing."

"Hey. I'm Tom." I don't know what else to say, and I just stand there for what seems like ages. Ryan seems a nice guy, and quite hot too. Good-looking, with an emo fringe, skinny jeans, and Converse. Normally, I'd be very interested in him, but just at the moment, he's in the way. I look across at Dan, who seems to pick up my slightly panicky expression, and steps forward.

"Hey, Ryan. Great to meet you. I'm Dan. Look, the thing is, mate, er, this is a bit difficult…" Ryan looks back and forth between the two of us, waiting for one of us to continue. "It's just that me and Tom, you know, we'd kind of agreed to share a room."

"What do you mean? What, this room?"

"Well, yeah, mate, if you don't mind."

Ryan looks very confused. "But they've just sent me to this room. I've got the key and all the paperwork and everything."

Dan struggles on. "Yeah, I know that, mate. It's not an official thing. I mean, we're in different rooms on the list, but we wanted to share, and we were going to use this room, because you hadn't arrived yet."

"Are you mates then? Did you go to the same school?"

"Well, no, not the same school, but we, er…" Oh God, this isn't going very well.

Ryan doesn't look happy at all. "Look. I've got everything unpacked. Well, nearly. I like this room. I don't see why it's so important for you, if you're not even mates or anything…"

I'm desperately trying to think what to say next, when Dan moves forward, looking confident. I think he's got an idea.

"Ryan, look, mate, I wasn't going to say this, because I didn't want to embarrass you or anything, but the thing is, we're, like, a couple."

It takes a few seconds before Ryan catches on. Fortunately, he looks at Dan not me, because my mouth drops open, and it takes me a moment to get my composure back.

"Shit. Oh sorry, I didn't realize. I see now."

"We should have said straightaway, but, you know, some people have a bit of a problem with it. I'm sure you won't, though?"

"No, course not. Look, I'm a bit of a, well, a bit emo. I suppose that's kind of obvious, really. You know what emos are like. Half my mates are lesbians or bisexuals or fucking... something!" I notice he doesn't use the "G" word.

"I knew you'd be cool about it."

"You're seriously, like, together, then? I mean, you don't look...Well, I know you can't always tell, but you're...well, I just wouldn't ever have guessed."

"Yeah, we've been together for about six months, isn't that right, Tom?"

I feel Dan coming up behind me, and then his arms are around my neck, and his head's right next to mine. I manage a reply. "Yeah, yeah, that's right."

Ryan's still not looking completely convinced. "This isn't a windup, is it?"

"We're still at that stage where we can't keep our hands off each other, you know what I mean?" Dan moves a hand down my body and grabs a handful of my crotch. He grabs me the way a pissed straight boy might grab his mate if they were fucking about. It's not an in-love couple sort of grab, but it seems to convince Ryan.

"Okay, guys, look, sorry, I wasn't...look, I wouldn't want to keep you two apart. I don't mind moving out."

"Ryan. You're sound, mate. Look, we owe you one."

"It's no problem."

"No, really. We owe you big time. Can we get you a beer or something? Do you want a spliff?" Out comes the bag of weed again. It seems ages since we were smoking down by the gardener's huts.

"Maybe later, eh. Cheers, though. I will take you up on that. But I think I'd better get my stuff packed up now. If I get wasted, I won't do it. Then there'll be three of us in here tonight, and I don't think you'll want an audience, eh?" Ryan gives us a very suggestive grin.

"Oh, I don't know. We could sell tickets." Dan puts his hand on my crotch again and then squeezes my bollocks. He really doesn't know how to do "loving touch" on a guy, and it hurts like fuck. I try not to show it, though.

Ryan laughs. "I'll pass on that one, okay?"

"Look, mate, shall we help you with your stuff?"

"No, it's fine. I'd rather do it myself. I know where everything is."

"You sure? We don't mind. Least we can do."

"It's okay. Look, you go off for a bit. Give me twenty minutes. That should be enough. I need you to come back, though. I don't know where my room's going to be."

"Well, if you're sure. We'll be back in a bit, then."

Neither of us speaks until we're right out of the accommodation block. Dan sets off down the path. "Bar. Come on. I need a pint." So do I! I can't believe what he's just done. Fortunately, the SU bars are just round the corner, and we're there in a couple of minutes. I get the drinks in, and we down them, standing at the bar. Dan calls the barman over and gets us another, and then we head off into the far corner, where it's fairly private. He swigs half of his second pint before he speaks.

"Shit."

"I know."

"I'm making him share with twat of the century, and he's such a nice bloke."

"What? Is that what you're thinking about?"

"What do you mean? Why? What are you thinking about?"

"Well, I'm thinking about how you've told him we're a couple."

"Oh that? It was the only thing I could think of."

"But—"

"It worked, didn't it?"

"Yeah, it worked. But what happens when he tells everyone that we're a couple? What are you going to do then? You going to admit you made it up?"

"I didn't think about that. I don't know what...well, I could..."

"Either that or you'll have to stay gay for the rest of the year."

"Fuck that."

"Which means you won't even get a sniff of pussy until you leave."

"And definitely fuck that. I'll tell him...I'll think of something. I'll say I've split up with you and turned straight from the shock. I don't know. It's all right. I'll think of something."

"You really don't care about anything do you?"

He looks suddenly serious. "Yeah, I do. I feel bad about lying to Ryan. He seemed like a sound bloke. I feel a proper cunt."

"Yeah. I know. We need to make it up to him if we can."

"Yeah." He picks up his beer again and downs the rest of it. "Anyway, you—you bastard. What the fuck is wrong with your dick?"

He's lost me completely. "Wrong?"

"Yeah. Does it stay hard twenty-four seven? I thought, you know, have a bit of a squeeze, like, convince Ryan we're for real, and I get a handful of fucking hard-on."

"Didn't stop you coming back for seconds, did it?"

"Fuck off. I was only doing it so Ryan would—"

"I know. It's all right."

"But you only had a wank about half an hour ago. I know, remember? I was there at the time."

I have a quick look down at my foot, where the wet stain on the lace of his trainers still shows. "I just stayed hard. It didn't go down. When I'm this horny, one wank isn't enough."

"You been hard all this time?"

"Well, not quite all the time. It went down a bit while we were walking over here. But it's back up now."

"Oh, for fuck's sake."

"What do you mean, 'For fuck's sake'? It's your fault I'm hard all the time."

"I haven't fucking done anything!"

"Yes, you have. Everything you do makes me more horny. You showed me the spunk in your bed, just to get me going. You let me wear your trainers, when you knew I had a thing about them. And then you felt my dick. In front of Ryan. Anyway, what happened to the no touching rule? You said no touching."

"Yeah, but that was just for you. You're not allowed to touch me. Well, not like that, anyway. Back there, it was me touching you, and that's allowed."

"Good. Well, you can do it again any time you want. You don't even need to ask, just go ahead."

"That was a one-off. Just because we needed to get Ryan to move out. Don't start expecting that—"

"Look, Dan. It's all right. I'm only winding you up. I know you're straight, and I'm not expecting anything. Okay?"

"Okay. So do you want another beer, or another wank?" The beer's gone straight to my head, actually. I've not had anything to eat, and I'm feeling a bit pissed already. But what the fuck?

"Can I have both? I don't think we've got time, though. We said we'd be back in twenty minutes. Shit."

"I don't know...Wait there." He's up and off to the bar. He's obviously got an idea, fuck knows what, though. I watch his arse as he gets more drinks, and keep watching him as he comes and sits back down. He's got a dirty smile on his face. "It's no good trying to get me wasted. It won't get you anywhere. Drink up then."

I pick up my pint and knock some of it back. Suddenly, there's something between my legs. Apart from what's normally there, obviously. I look down, and Dan's leg is between mine, with his foot sliding into place in my crotch. He's got his leg stretched out under the little round table that's between us.

"Dan! What you doing? You can't. Not here."

"Shut up and drink your beer." I try to drink some more, but he's started rubbing his foot up and down, and it's hard not to spill it. Then he presses his foot harder against my cock, and it feels nice. It feels very nice.

"What if someone sees us? Dan, we're in the middle of a bar."

"No one's going to see because there's hardly anyone here. And we're not in the middle; we're in a nice, private little corner." His foot goes back to rubbing up and down. The friction gets a response from my nob straightaway. But we can't do this. It's madness.

"It doesn't feel very private to me, Dan. We're going to get caught."

"Tell me to stop then."

"What?"

"Tell me to stop."

I open my mouth and then shut it again. I want to say it. I should say it. Of course, I should. But I'm not going to. And he knows I'm not going to. I can't. I put my beer down on the table and open my legs a bit wider. Then I look down. Dan's foot is kind of massaging my cock, and it feels amazing. He's wearing my trainers of course; big, padded skate trainers, and the sole is pressed hard against me. My breathing quickens, and I take hold of the table with both hands to steady myself against the effects of the beer and the waves of excitement and lust that are already starting to take control of me.

I keep a firm hold on the table, fix my eyes on Dan's foot, and give in to the building orgasm that's going to break over me any second. My breath is coming in gasps, and I'm tensing my muscles to push back against his foot. Then, just before I get past the point of no return, he stops moving. I'm right on the edge. I need to cum so badly. I open my mouth to say something, to beg him to keep going, but he stops me. "Shh. No talking."

Then I see the bottom of his jeans leg starting to move up. He's got his hands under the table, where I can't see them, but he must be pulling at the denim because, very slowly, I'm starting to see more of his leg. First, just enough to lift away from my trainer and show a glimpse of white sports sock. Then, gradually, I can see more of his sock, right up to the three black lines round the top. I'm in a state of suspended animation, right on the edge of cumming. Hardly breathing. Why is this so hot? He's only showing me his leg, for fuck's sake. But I want to see it. Come on, a bit higher now, and I can see his leg coming into view, tanned, muscly, and covered in dark hair.

I don't think about what I'm doing. I can't think; I'm too fucking horny. I make a grab for his leg with both hands. My right hand goes onto his ankle, taking hold of his sock, and my left hand slides down inside the trainer to hold his foot. I never do the laces of my trainers up properly, so they're loose and I can get my hand in easily. As soon as I feel the shape of his foot and the sweat on his sock, I'm cumming. I hold tightly to his leg and grind my dick hard into the sole of the trainer. Fuck, it hurts, but I don't care. The first few blasts of cum start shooting into my boxers. I'm gasping for breath, and my legs are shaking uncontrollably.

Somewhere in the back of my mind, I know I'm making too much noise. I should keep it down, or someone will hear. But I can't. It's just too intense.

As my orgasm builds, I slide my right hand up onto his leg, running it through the hair and over the tight muscle. I grind his foot even harder against my dick, as it throbs and squirts. He's just letting me do what I want with his leg, and it feels incredible.

Eventually, it begins to subside a bit. I look up at Dan, and we lock eyes. He's still got the dirty smile on his face. I'm too exhausted to smile, completely out of breath, my chest rising and falling like I've just done a marathon or something.

I keep hold of Dan's foot until my orgasm has properly finished and I'm beginning to get my breath back. He's seems happy to wait. Then in the end, I let go, and he moves his leg away.

"Dan, you shouldn't have done that. It was fucking insane."

"Finish your beer. We've got to go." I do as I'm told. Shit, I feel dizzy. Now all that lust is draining away, I'm feeling the effects of the beer even more.

"I'm a bit pissed. Sorry."

"Sorry you're pissed?"

"No. Sorry I grabbed your leg. I didn't mean to. I said I wouldn't."

"Yeah, you did, didn't you? But I suppose I did lead you on just a bit."

"Just a bit."

"So I suppose it was slightly my fault too."

"Just slightly."

"And it was a laugh."

"It was fucking incredible."

The big grin is back on his face, and he puts his empty glass down on the table. "Right. I'm desperate for a piss. You've made me have three pints, you cunt. You're such a bad influence."

I put my best serious face on. "I'm really sorry, Dan. It won't happen again."

He laughs. "It better not. Right, I've got three pints of piss to get rid of, and I expect you'll want to watch."

"What? I...that's so unfair. You seem to think I'm some kind of..." It's no good. I just give in. "Yes. I want to watch. Of course I fucking want to watch."

"That's okay then. Let's go. Ryan will be waiting for us."

Chapter Three

We get up together and head for the toilet, the same one where I had my last-but-one orgasm. Christ, was that only an hour ago?

I try to remember what it's like in there. I think there's one of those long metal piss troughs along one wall, and the two cubicles opposite. It's only the cubicles I can remember properly, but I suppose that's understandable. I wonder if Dan will head for a cubicle, where we can lock ourselves in, or go for the piss trough, which would be more dangerous, but maybe more exciting.

Dan pushes the door open, and we go in. Fuck! There are two blokes standing there, pissing. Now what do we do? There's plenty of room at the long trough, so it will look really odd if we just wait here until they finish. One of the guys looks over his shoulder at us, and then looks down again.

Dan seems to hesitate for a second, and then pushes open the door to the second cubicle. What's he doing? We can't both go in together, not with these other blokes in here, and he said I could watch. But he doesn't get past the doorway.

"What the fuck?" Dan steps back, registering an impressive mixture of surprise and disgust. "Look what some cunt's done in here."

I look in over his shoulder. I was expecting that my cum would have dried by now, but there it is, still shiny against the dark tiled floor and partition wall. "Jesus, that's fucking disgusting."

By now, one of the guys has finished at the urinal, and comes across. "What's going on, mate?"

Dan screws up his face, like there's a bad smell somewhere. "Some fucker's spunked in here, mate. It's all over everywhere."

"The dirty bastard. Sam," he calls to the other guy, who's finished pissing and is doing up his fly. "Some fucker's spunked all over the floor."

Sam comes over and gives it a quick look. "That's gross. What's wrong with some people? For fuck's sake." As they leave, they're still discussing it. They'll probably be discussing it all day.

Thank God. They've gone. Now I can get my first look at Dan's nob. I'm so desperate to see it, I can't wait! I'm at the urinal and undoing my belt and jeans in a couple of seconds. Dan saunters across slowly and stands next to me.

"Come on. Please. I want to see it."

I hope he isn't going to be a twat and start teasing me by getting it out really slowly. I'm afraid that's the kind of thing he might enjoy doing.

Shit. He is. He puts his hands behind his head, and starts stretching and yawning. My stream of piss starts, quite slowly at first, but then it's like someone turned on a tap. Three pints of beer, straight in and straight out.

Dan's still stretching and posing, and I've waited long enough. "Dan. Stop fucking around. Point your dick at this wall right now, or I'll piss all over you!"

"Easy, tiger. I'm doing it. Chill, okay?" He starts to undo his jeans and I move a little closer, until our trainers are touching.

Then he gives the front of his boxers a bit of a rub with his hand, and his fingers go under the waistband and pull it down. I expect I'm still pissing, but there's only one thing I'm aware of right now, and it's the long tube that's appearing over the top of Dan's boxers, having his right hand wrapped round it and starting to produce a stream of almost clear piss.

Soon he's pissing so hard that there's a lot of it splashing back off the metal piss trough. I can feel a fine spray hitting my hand and my cock starts to harden a bit. I hold it loosely and let it grow, feeling my bell-end pushing forward and out through my foreskin. Suddenly, Dan's foreskin is pulling back too! Holy shit! I can't tell if he's pulling it back, or if he's getting hard too. I don't actually care. I'm just standing here watching him, and that's all I need at the moment. I'm so pleased we had that third pint; it means that he just keeps on pissing. I'm loving it, and I think he's having a good time too. He starts swinging his cock from side to side, making the stream of piss snake backward and forward, like water from a hose.

Then he turns to face me more. He can see how excited I'm getting, and I suppose he wants to give me a better view. His piss is shooting across in front of me now, very close to where the last drops are falling from my semi-hard bell-end. I don't even think about whether I should or not. I just do it. I push my hips forward a few inches and dip my bell-end into the hot stream. His piss runs over the shiny tightness of my bell and drips off into the urinal. I'm transfixed. I just stand there watching until he's completely finished, and then I remember to start breathing again.

Now he's shaking it dry, and pushing his foreskin forward and back until the last drop is gone. It's not properly hard, but it's definitely not soft either. There's a bit of firmness to it, and I'm wondering how much bigger it will get later on, when the porn is doing its job on it. Oh God, I can't wait.

I snap out of my dream world as Dan's dick disappears into his boxers, and he starts to do up his jeans. I quickly follow suit, stuffing my nearly hard one into my cold, wet, cummy boxers.

Dan looks at me. I think he's trying not to smile. "I thought you were perverted when we came in here the first time. But that was nothing compared to this." Yes! He's going to start the insults again. I loved it when he did that last time. "You ought to be fucking locked away. You're not safe round normal people."

"Normal like you, you mean?"

"Yeah, mate. Normal like me."

"You pissed on my bell-end. It's you that's not normal."

"You put your bell-end in the way of my piss, you dirty queer bastard."

"And you wanked me off, straight boy. In public!"

"Did I fuck."

"Yeah, you did."

"You wanked yourself off, mate. You just used my shoe. Actually, it wasn't even my shoe. You wanked yourself off using your own shoe, because, in case you've forgotten, I'm wearing your trainers, because you masturbated on mine about five minutes after you first met me."

I've completely run out of insults, but it's my turn to say something. "Well, you enjoyed it as well, and you're supposed to be straight."

Dan smiles, and thinks for a second. "Well, let's see, shall we?" He comes over and stands right in front of me. One of his hands grabs his own belt, and the other grabs mine, pulling them away from our bodies. Dan looks carefully, first into his own boxers, then mine. "Well, it looks like you enjoyed it a whole lot more than I did!"

Suddenly, the toilet door slams open and a short, stocky guy in a tracksuit appears. It happens so suddenly that there isn't any time to take avoiding action. We are blatantly looking down each other's pants. Tracksuit guy says, "Shit." and makes a run for it. He's gone as quickly as he appeared.

Dan doesn't look bothered. "Well, he should fucking knock before he comes into a room. Then he wouldn't get nasty surprises." We both crack up.

We head out of the SU building and Dan turns the wrong way. I have to remind him which room we're going to, and it takes him a few seconds to get his head round it.

"Dan, are you pissed?"

"Tom, mate, I'm off my fucking tits. I've had three spliffs and three pints today already, and I haven't eaten a fucking thing."

"Well, don't say anything stupid in front of Ryan." As soon as I've said it, I want to take it back. Telling Dan not to say something stupid, and when he's pissed up too. He could do anything!

"Mate, don't worry. It's all safe." I think I'll try to do most of the talking when we get back to the room. I'm feeling the effects of the beer, but I'm not in as bad a state as Dan.

Dan's still laughing at the look on tracksuit guy's face when we get back to my room, where we left Ryan packing his stuff. I find the key and let us in. Ryan is sitting on the bed playing with his phone, and he gets up as soon as we come in.

"I thought you weren't coming." He looks genuinely worried. "I thought you'd just pissed off and weren't coming back."

I step forward. "Sorry, Ryan. Are we late?"

Ryan looks at his phone. "Yeah, a bit. It's about an hour."

"Shit. An hour? Sorry."

"A bit more, actually. It's all right. Don't worry about it."

I sense Dan moving forward, and there's nothing I can do to stop whatever he's going to say. "Actually, mate, it was all Tom's fault."

Fuck. Where's this going?

"Yeah, he made me go to the bar and get really fucking pissed."

"Dan..."

"I was only going to have one, but he kept buying more fucking beer, so I had to drink it. I told him we had to go, because we said twenty minutes, and you'd be waiting. I said, 'Ryan will be fucking waiting, Tom,' but he wouldn't fucking listen to me, Ryan, mate. You know what I mean?"

Dan's slurring his words a bit, and it is actually quite funny, but I'm not going to let him get away with it. "Ryan, this is all bullshit. You do know that, don't you?"

But Dan isn't finished. "And then he made me wank him off."

"Dan, shut up, for fuck's sake."

"We were just going, and he says 'Dan, wank me off. I'm fucking desperate for one.'"

"Dan! Christ. Sorry. Ryan, he's a bit pissed."

"He's a dirty cunt, you know? He might look fucking innocent, but he's dirty as fuck."

I look over at Ryan, who's got a big smile on his face, and looks like he's fine with all this. But I'm not sure. I'm worried that he may be quite embarrassed and covering it up. I think I'd better rescue him before Dan says anything else.

"Dan. You say another word and I'm going to fucking punch you or something."

Dan puts his finger to his lips and makes a little "Shh" sound. It's so cute, I want to snog his face off. Fuck. Don't think about that. Need to go. Need to get Ryan sorted out and then get back...

"Right. Dan, you stay here, and I'll help Ryan with his stuff."

"Yeah, yeah. I'll stay here. I'm a bit pissed, actually, Ryan, mate."

"I think he's noticed that."

"I'll get the porn set up while you're out." I just give up. There's no point saying anything. I just look at Ryan and wait to see what's coming next. "Because we're having a fucking dirty porn wankathon later, aren't we, Tom?" He turns to Ryan. "You into porn, mate?"

Ryan's definitely okay with that question, and his smile gets even bigger. "Yeah, I love it. Watch loads."

"What sort of stuff are you into, mate?"

"Oh, you know, anything. Just normal stuff."

"Yeah, normal stuff. Just so long as it's proper fucking dirty." Dan's starting to get into this, and I'm thinking that he's going to forget that he's supposed to be gay in a minute.

I leap in. "Normal gay stuff, obviously. I mean, not the kind of stuff Ryan watches, I don't expect."

Dan *has* forgotten! For a split second, his face is absolutely blank, and then he suddenly registers. "Yeah, normal gay stuff, obviously. You know, men fucking other men." For fuck's sake. Is that the best he can do? That wouldn't convince anyone. Well, the whole "pretending to be gay" thing was Dan's idea, so if he fucks it up, he'll have to get himself out of it.

Right; second attempt to get us out of here. I look over at Ryan. "You all set, then?"

"Yeah. Think so."

"Thanks for doing this, Ryan. You know, swapping rooms and everything."

"It's no problem."

Dan comes over too. "Yeah, cheers, mate. You're a fucking legend."

I pick up a box and a bag. Ryan doesn't seem to have much stuff, and we're soon out of the door. "Ryan, is this seriously all you brought with you?"

"Yeah, but I've got some more stuff coming on Sunday. My mum doesn't have a car, so she's got to wait until the weekend when she can borrow our next-door neighbor's."

I wonder what Ryan's home life has been like; not as easy as mine, by the sound of it.

He looks across at me as we go down the stairs. "So how much of that was true, then?"

Oh shit. He's worked it out. It was probably Dan's lame attempt to describe gay porn that did it. I hedge. "What do you mean?"

"Did you really make him, you know?" He makes a wanking gesture with his hand.

"No! He just, well, I suppose I did say I wanted one. But I didn't make him. That was bullshit. He likes to wind people up."

"It's all right. I *thought* you'd gone off to have sex."

"What?"

"When you said you were going to piss off for a bit, I thought you'd go and have sex somewhere."

So he hasn't worked it out at all. He's still buying the whole "gay couple" thing. Perhaps Dan isn't as unconvincing as I thought. Or maybe Ryan just accepts things. Not everyone overanalyzes everything all the time like I do.

We're inside Ryan's block now, and as we climb the stairs, he asks, "What's the guy like who I'm sharing with? What's his name?"

Shit. Another question I don't want to answer. "Well, I don't remember his name. I only met him for a few seconds. Just to say hi to, you know?"

"Did he seem okay?"

"Hard to say, really. Like I say, I only saw him for a few seconds." I'm praying that geek boy won't be in, and as Ryan turns the key and swings the door open, I scan the room. Thank fuck for that. No sign of him. We go in, and Ryan does a quick tour of the room. It doesn't take long; there's not much to look at, and he puts the box he's carrying down on the bed.

The bed is exactly as Dan and I left it. Oh shit! The duvet's still on the floor and the sheet is still covered with the evidence of Dan's nighttime activities and my daytime ones. Ryan's standing looking at the big wet circle on the sheet. Then he sits on the bed and peers at it more closely.

"I don't suppose this is anything to do with you and Dan, is it?" There's a slight smirk on Ryan's face. He's obviously not slow at picking up on some things.

"Ah, well, er, Dan slept in this room last night, and he needed to, you know, squirt some juice and, er, so he did, and…" I can't tell him the other bit. Fuck. I'd die if he knew about that. "And then, when we knew we were swapping rooms, we, er, tried to wash it out with some water."

"Really?"

"Yeah. Look, Ryan, I'll take that sheet off and change it. I'll get one from our room or somewhere."

I move forward to grab the sheet, but Ryan stops me. "It's all right, I'll do it."

"No, look. I should. I mean, we made the mess in the first place, well, Dan did, and we shouldn't have just left it for you to find. It's a bit bad. Well, it's fucking gross, actually. I suppose, it's not like Dan was wanking in your room, because it wasn't your room then, but it still feels, fucking…fucking…"

"I said it's all right. I'll sort it out in a bit." He looks at me from under his fringe and grins. "Anyway, I had a wank in your room, so I guess we're even."

"What? When?"

"When you were at the bar. It only took about five minutes to pack my stuff, and I got bored. I watched some porn on my phone, and, well, you know…"

"What if we'd come back? Weren't you worried about us catching you?"

"No. I knew you'd be ages. I was pretty sure you'd gone off for a fuck anyway."

"You dirty bastard! You're as bad as me. I didn't think you'd be like that. Leave you alone for five minutes and you're whacking off over phone porn."

"Actually, it wasn't…" There's a change in Ryan's body language, he kind of stiffens up, and takes two very deep breaths. I wonder what he's psyching himself up to say. "It wasn't so much the porn."

"Ryan, what's up?"

"It wasn't the porn that got me, you know, horny. Well, it was a bit. But mostly it was thinking about you two."

"You were thinking about me and Dan?"

"Yeah. Having sex."

Oh, fuck. How much more complicated can this get?

"You got turned on thinking about me and Dan having sex?"

"Yeah."

"Do you, I mean, is that the sort of thing you normally get, you know, turned on by?"

"Sometimes. Well, more than sometimes." He's looking really awkward and uncomfortable.

"Fucking hell. So you're what? Gay or bi or what?"

There's quite a long pause while Ryan looks down and doesn't make eye contact. "Look, Tom. I'm sorry. I'm finding this hard. Harder than I thought I would."

"Don't worry. You don't have to talk about it if it's difficult."

"I was going to do this ages ago, back in sixth form. And then, I was going to tell people at the leavers' prom. I had it all planned out. But it didn't happen."

"That's all right. It's difficult. I know that."

"Then I thought I'd tell everyone here, you know, straightaway. But I couldn't do that either. I wanted to tell you two. It should have been easy, because you're gay, and you'd be fine with it, but I couldn't even do that. Fuck!" Ryan's head drops forward and he looks really miserable.

"Ryan, it's fine. Don't worry about it. You've told me about it now, so that's a start."

"I feel like I've gone backward in my head. I was all set and ready to come out. I was feeling quite confident, you know? I'd been talking to a guy on Gay Switchboard, and people online, and I was ready, you know? But I've lost all my confidence about it now."

"Why? Did something happen?"

He stops and looks up at me, a strange, rather bleak look that really unsettles me. He obviously wants to say more, and I make myself sit silently and wait until he's ready. Eventually, it comes. "I had a bad experience."

"Shit."

"I've been trying to, you know, shut it out, not think about it, but it's not—"

"Not working?"

"Tom. Can I ask you something? You can tell me to fuck off if you want."

"Just say it. Whatever it is. I won't mind."

"How much is it supposed to hurt when you get fucked?"

Shit! How the fuck should I know that? I've got to say something, though. I'll just have to throw together various things I've picked up from websites and stories, and from watching porn. That's the best I can do. "Well, I suppose, well, it's hard to say really. I mean, it depends on a lot of things."

"What about when—" He stops and looks up at me again from under the fringe. I know what's coming. "What about when it's happening to you? I mean, with Dan, when you…the first time, was it really bad?"

"No, no, it was…" Fuck. What do I say? "I guess we just took it really slowly, and…no, it was fine." Fuck. Fuck. Fuck. I don't think I can keep this up any more. I'm going to have to tell him the truth. He seems such a nice guy. It's not fair to let this go on any longer. Besides, sitting so close to him for this long has given me the chance to have a proper look at him, and he is really nice-looking. And now I know he's probably gay as well. I know what I need to say. It's just finding the right words.

As I open my mouth to speak, I see a tear running down Ryan's nose, and then another. Shit, he's really upset about this. I can't tell him now. "Ryan, what's the matter? Mate? Is it something I said?' He shakes his head, and the tears drip onto the floor. "Do you want to talk about whatever it is?"

He's openly crying now, and compulsively twisting the ring he's wearing on his thumb. The silence lengthens between us, and I really don't know what to do. The thought comes into my head that I should put my arm around him, or give him a hug, or something, but even as I'm thinking it, I start overanalyzing again. I only want to hug him because I fancy him, not because I feel sorry for him. But surely, I'm not…So what do I do? I can't just carry on like nothing's wrong. Think. If I were straight, what would I do? What would Dan do? I decide that Dan would definitely put his arm round him. It's the right thing to do. If I enjoy doing it, that doesn't matter. It's still the right thing to do.

I move closer to Ryan on the bed and put my arm round his shoulders. I can feel his shoulder bones through his T-shirt.

I can't help glancing down his back to where there's a big gap between his T-shirt and the top of his jeans, which are very low on his hips. I can just about see right down to where his arse crack starts. Fuck. I'm not supposed to be getting off on this. I switch my gaze back up and give his shoulder a squeeze. I'm hoping it will help to make him feel better, but instead he seems to cry more, his body shaking and shivering. I put my other hand onto the leg of his jeans and give his leg a gentle rub. Now my eyes go straight to the really big bulge in his jeans. His skinny jeans are so tight, there's no way of hiding anything in them, and Ryan's obviously got plenty in there. I can't tell if it's hard or soft though, which is frustrating. Fuck. I've got to stop doing this. This time I have to force myself to look away, and to look at his face. "Come on, Ryan, why don't you just tell me the whole thing? You'll feel better once you've told someone."

After a few seconds, Ryan nods his head, sniffs a couple of times, and wipes his face with his hands. Then he puts his hand down on top of my hand and closes his fingers round mine. His hand is wet with his tears. "You don't mind if I do this, do you?"

At last, a question I can just give an honest answer to. "Course I don't mind. It's fine. It feels nice." I close my arm a little tighter round his shoulder.

"Okay." He takes a deep breath. "There was this guy, you see. I was at Rock Garden, and he—"

"Hang on. What's Rock Garden?"

"Oh, it's a club. A live music place; rock bands, you know. I saw this guy there, and he kept looking at me and following me around. I quite liked him, you know, and he must have seen I was looking back at him. When the band came on, he got right behind me and was like, grinding against me. He was really hard, and so was I, and then he put his hand in my pocket, and started rubbing my dick. I got so turned on."

"First time anything like that had happened to you?"

"Yeah. In the end, he said he'd take me round the back, and we could have some fun. I was so horny, I just went with him. When we got out of sight, he just sort of changed. He went really aggressive. He shoved me hard up against the wall and just started trying to stick it in me. It hurt so much. It felt like I was going to die. I started shouting for him to stop, but he didn't. He just put his hand over my mouth and tried to carry on. In the end, I grabbed his balls and squeezed them quite hard. I managed to kind of fight him off. He was really angry. He banged my head against the wall and called me a prick-teasing little cunt."

"Shit, Ryan. Fucking hell. No wonder you've lost your confidence. Shit." Ryan's still quite shaky, but he seems to have stopped crying. I'm not sure what to say next. "Look, it doesn't have to be like that. The guy you met was a bastard, a sicko. Most guys aren't like that."

"I know. But he scared me."

"You just need to meet a really nice guy. You'll be able to get over this."

"Do you think I'm gay then?"

"Shit, Ryan, I don't know. I mean, do you ever think about girls? Like fantasies, I mean? You've told me you think about guys sometimes, and you were thinking about me and Dan, weren't you? But I can't see inside your head. If you *were* gay, how would you...I mean, would you have a problem with it?"

"I don't know. I don't fucking know about anything anymore. I've tried to shut it all out. After what happened, I tried to stop thinking about guys, but it all keeps fucking coming back."

"Ryan, it's not good to block things out. It fucks with your head. And anyway, you can't keep things blocked out forever."

"I've realized that."

"You're going to have to be honest about what you really want, sometime. It won't be easy, but you'll go mad otherwise."

"There's no point in me being honest about what I want. Not now, anyway."

Suddenly, I've lost track of where this conversation is heading. "I don't get you. What do you mean?"

"There's no point wanting something you can't have, is there?"

"Ryan, I still haven't got a clue what you're on about."

There's another long silence, and I feel Ryan's body shaking. Then the tears start again, and he says in a very small voice, "I knew something like this would happen. I knew one day I'd meet a really nice guy who I really liked, and he'd be…he'd be…going out with someone else already."

Is he saying? Fuck. No. Ryan wants…and he thinks… Fuck! This can't be happening. Shit. Think. Shit. "Ryan, are you saying? Fucking hell. Look, are you saying you want…do you mean me?"

Ryan seems to break down completely. He's sobbing and crying so much that I can hardly make out his words. "I'm sorry. I didn't mean to. I shouldn't have said anything. I know you and Dan…and he's so nice…you're both so nice. Why did I have to fucking say that?"

"Ryan, don't worry. It's all right, really."

"It's not all right. I've fucked everything up as usual."

I slide forward off the bed and kneel in front of Ryan. Taking hold of his shoulders, I lift him up so he's looking at me. "Ryan. I want you to listen to me, okay? Come on, stop crying." I look around for something to wipe his eyes with, but there's nothing obvious to use so I pull my hoodie off over my head and dab at his eyes with the sleeve. He lets me do it for a few seconds, and then finishes the job himself. I reach up and brush his fringe across, out of his eyes. He's looking very red and blotchy, but he's stopped crying, and his eyes are fixed on mine.

"First off, you haven't fucked anything up. You've said what you feel, and that's good. I mean that's positive, isn't it? And I, well, I think I kind of feel…shit, I've told you that you need to be honest about what you feel, and now I can't fucking say what I want to." I take a deep breath. "I think you're a really hot guy, and to be honest, I'm having a hard time keeping my hands off you."

"But you're…"

"Yeah, I know. But me and Dan, we, er, well, we don't have…it's not that kind of relationship. We can do what we like, kind of."

"Seriously?"

"Yeah. It's a pretty unusual, er, relationship, but it's fine."

I run my hands through his hair again and wipe away a last stray tear with my thumb. This is surreal. "So anything you want to do is fine with me. I'd love it. Seriously. But I'm not going to start anything unless you're sure you want to, okay? It's up to you. If you want me to go now, so you can think about things, that's fine, but if you want me to stay, that's fine too."

"Don't go. I don't want you to go. I want…will you just hold me for a bit?"

I shuffle forward on my knees until I'm as close to the bed as I can get, and reach out to him. Ryan moves forward to the edge of the bed and throws both arms around me, pulling me in toward him. I close my arms around his back, and we don't move for what seems like ages, just squeezing and holding and breathing together.

My head is pressed to Ryan's chest, and I'm drinking in the smell of him, a mixture of sweat, aftershave, and an indefinable man smell. It's nice, but not as nice as what I'm feeling lower down. Ryan's legs are open wide on either side of me, and my stomach is pressed hard against his crotch, where his cock is throbbing and straining inside the tight jeans. I can feel the shape of it, the hardness of it. I think I can even feel it twitch, with every heartbeat, through the tightly stretched denim.

Eventually, I allow my hand to move up his back, and I run it through his hair. "Ryan, are you all right?"

"Yeah. I think so. I've never done anything like this before, you know."

I want to tell him that I haven't either; that this is new and exciting and amazing for me too, but of course I can't. I will explain everything to him, but not now. "It doesn't matter. Are you still feeling scared?"

"Kind of scared. I think it's more excited than scared though."

"Yeah. I can feel how excited you are."

"Oh shit. Sorry."

"For God's sake, Ryan, don't apologize for getting a boner. I'm fucking loving it!" He laughs, and I feel the movement from it go through his body. "You can keep it there all day if you like."

"I don't think I could."

"What? Why not?"

"It really hurts, actually."

"Oh, Ryan. You should have said before. Do you want me to move?"

"No, no please. It isn't you. It's these jeans. They're so tight, when I get, you know, a boner, it fucking kills."

I'm just going to go for it. Why the fuck not? "You'd better get it out then."

"Fucking hell. Seriously?"

"Yeah. I mean, only if you want to. I don't want to push you into doing anything."

"Of course I want to. I really want to."

"That's cool then. I could help you get those jeans undone. That would be really hot. And I can help you with some other stuff too, but only if you're sure you want me to."

"What stuff?"

"Well, I was thinking that if it's my fault you're hard in there, I should maybe help to get it soft again." I find myself grinning like a fucking monkey while I'm saying this, but I just can't help it. It's all too exciting. I look up and Ryan's grinning too, so I think it's going to happen.

"I've never got my nob out in front of anyone before; not when it's hard, I mean."

"Is that what you want to happen now?"

"Oh God, yeah."

"Lie back on the bed then." I put my hand on Ryan's chest and push him gently, and he allows himself to fall back onto the bed. He reaches for his fly, but I put out my hand to stop him. "Let me do it. Please."

I run my hand over his crotch again, tracing the shape of his dick, bent round and trapped in the tight fabric. I undo the buttons on his jeans, and pull the fly wide open. His dick straightens up immediately, circling round under the thin material of his boxers, until it comes to rest, caught under the waistband. I watch it for a few seconds as it jumps and twitches, and then I put my hand into the top of his boxers and pull them away from his body. His dick snaps upright, quivering a little, the foreskin pulled right back and a smear of pre-cum glistening on the bell-end. I rub my finger gently along his piss-slit, and feel him stiffen. Another big drop of pre-cum oozes out, and he raises himself onto his elbows and looks at me.

"Ryan, I want to make you cum. I want to so fucking much. But I'm not going to do anything unless you say it's all right."

"Yeah, do it. Please. I want you to."

I know exactly what I'm going to do. I'm going to suck Ryan's dick. Somehow, it doesn't matter that I've never done it before; I know it'll be instinctive. I've watched it happening on a screen, hundreds of times, and imagined doing it more often than that. Now it's going to happen.

My cock is so hard it's almost hurting me, but it doesn't feel right to get it out. I want this time to be just for Ryan. Dan's told me what I can expect when I get back to our room, and I'm going to save my cum until then.

That doesn't mean I can't enjoy this to the full, though. I run my hand down Ryan's leg and over his rather sexy Converse. I take hold of his ankle, and lift his leg, putting the thin sole of his trainer right against my cock. "Can you feel that? Can you feel my hard-on?"

His foot moves inside the shoe, and presses against me. "Yeah, I can feel it. You're fucking dirty, you know."

"Yeah. And you're fucking sexy." I close my legs to keep his foot trapped against my boner, and move my head toward his bell-end. Wrapping my hand round his cock, I pull it down toward me and lick right across the top. The pre-cum slides off onto my tongue, but it's quickly replaced by some more. Ryan makes a groaning noise. He's so turned on I think he's going to cum really fast, and I want to make sure it's a good one.

I open my mouth and let his bell-end slide inside. It feels bigger than I thought it would. It isn't uncomfortable; it feels great actually, but I wasn't expecting my mouth to feel this full. I start to move my tongue against the underside of his bell-end. It's a place that's supersensitive on my own cock, so I think Ryan will like it. Judging by the noises he's making, he's loving it. I push it a bit further into my mouth and then suck in my cheeks and pull out and back in. I've only been doing it for a few seconds when there's another groan from

Ryan, and as I pull it out and back in again, I feel his whole cock change shape in my mouth, bigger, tighter, harder. All his muscles tense up, and his foot presses harder against me. "Shit, Tom, I—"

Before he can even finish, the first jet of cum slams into the back of my mouth. His hips jerk hard, which forces the tip of his cock hard into my throat, firing the second blast into me, almost making me choke. He keeps up the thrusting, each thrust delivering a bit more of his massive load, and he keeps thrusting even after the supply of juice is completely exhausted. I just about manage to keep my mouth closed round his cock until he finishes cumming. Eventually, he falls back onto the bed, panting and gasping for breath.

My mouth feels like it's completely full of cum. I've swallowed quite a lot, and I can feel a bit dribbling down my chin, but there's still loads in my mouth. He must have shot fucking gallons of the stuff. I swallow. It's not the first time I've swallowed cum, obviously, but it's the first time I've swallowed anyone else's. It tastes nice, hot and thick, and knowing how much passion and lust Ryan put into shooting it, makes it taste even better.

I look back at Ryan, lying flat out on the bed, his chest rising and falling. He needs a bit longer to come down from his orgasm, so I take the opportunity to slip my hands inside his Converse, closing my fingers under his feet and feeling the damp warmth and sweatiness on my hands. Oh, fuck. This is so hot.

With my hands still in his trainers, I lean forward again, to lick the last of the cum off his dick. When he feels my tongue, Ryan raises himself up on his elbows and smiles. I smile back.

"Feeling better now?" He nods, and his smile gets bigger. "But look. You know I'm going to have to leave soon and go back to Dan's? Will you still be okay then?"

There's a pause. I can see he's struggling for a moment, but then he seems to make a decision. "Well, I'd rather you stayed here, you know, just stayed here and never left, but I know that's stupid, so when you go, I'm going to lie here and imagine the last ten minutes over and over again. Then I'm probably going to watch every bit of porn I've got on my phone, wank myself stupid, and then drink until I throw up over myself and pass out in a pool of vomit." But he's still managing a smile as he says it.

"So you'll be all right, then?"

"I will if you promise you'll come back tomorrow."

"Of course I'll come back tomorrow. If you really want me to." Suddenly, Ryan grabs my face with both hands, and kisses me full on the mouth. It's so unexpected that I don't have time to respond. It's over in a second.

Ryan opens his mouth to speak. I just know he's going to say sorry again. "Ryan, don't you fucking dare apologize." This time it's me taking hold of Ryan's face and moving in to kiss him. And this time it doesn't end; we stay locked together, and my tongue pushes its way between his lips and into the warm wetness of his mouth, and our hands are rubbing and exploring each other's bodies, and all the feelings we've been holding back for so long rush to the surface and take us over.

Eventually, we unlock our tongues and mouths, and disentangle arms and bodies. I brush Ryan's fringe across, out of his eyes, and touch his cheek with my hand. "Are you sure you'll be okay?"

"Course I will."

"I'll see you tomorrow."

"Promise?"

"Promise."

CHAPTER FOUR

I t takes a bit longer to leave Ryan's room than I thought it would. First, we have to exchange phone numbers, and then we need to snog each other again at the door. Our hands are all over each other, Ryan's feeling up my dick. He wants to suck it, he says, and I'm desperate for it. But I know I should get back to Dan. Half an hour ago, I was desperate for *him,* and now I'm in danger of just dropping him to stay with Ryan.

I promise Ryan once again that we'll meet up tomorrow, and he can do whatever he wants to me. I think he's okay with it, although I can tell he's disappointed. One last kiss, and then I'm going through the door and setting off for my room, where I know Dan's getting the porn set up.

On the way, I scroll through my photos, and find the best one I have of my nob. I like this one, because you can see some pre-cum, and, to be honest, it's a flattering angle and it makes my meat look bigger than it actually is.

I'm just sending it to Ryan as I emerge from the stairwell onto my corridor. I stop outside the door to put my phone away, and I'm immediately aware of voices inside our room. Shit. Who's in there? I hope they're not staying long. Dan's promised me porn and a cum-shot, and that's what I'm fucking getting! I open the door and step inside.

The sight that greets me is fucking incredible. Dan hasn't got anyone else in the room with him. He's on his own and talking to someone on his webcam.

He's pushed the two beds together in the far corner of the room, and he's sitting on one of them, facing me. His laptop is on the bed between his legs, with the webcam clipped to the top of the screen.

He's totally naked, and his body is fucking amazing. I can see the whole of his chest, slim and quite tanned, with a bit of hair running down the center. I can see the whole of his legs, muscly and hairy, with the soles of his feet pointing toward me, and his toes flexing and straightening.

I can see his arm moving too, in that all too familiar movement that can only mean one thing.

But I can't see the most important bit. The laptop screen's in the fucking way. Not for long though. I step forward into the room and move round to where I can get a full, uninterrupted view, and it's well worth it. His cock is fat and quite long. It's not one of those freak-sized ones you see sometimes on porn websites, but it's big, and it's beautiful. Just the right size to suck, just the right size to get your hand round and wank. Fuck, I'm so horny again! And I'm so desperate to do all the stuff I promised Dan I wouldn't do. Shit. How has it got so complicated already?

Dan looks up at me and gives me the dirty boy smile that I'm already growing to love. "So where the fuck have you been? Thought you were only going to be a few minutes. I've needed to cum for fucking ages, you know, but it's okay, I've waited until you got here. I've been leaking pre-cum like a motherfucker, though." He looks down to his right, where one of his white sports socks is crumpled up next to him. Yes! Spunky sports sock. I'm having that.

I'm a bit distracted by the sock and don't reply straightaway. He asks again, "So what took you so long?" I get a flashback of Ryan's cum exploding into the back of my mouth and feel myself breaking into a grin. "Tom? Did something kick off with you and—" My face gives me away. "Fucking hell, mate. It did, didn't it? You dirty cunt."

"I'm still ready for some porn."

"What? Are you still up for it?"

"Fuck, yeah! Look, I'll tell you everything later, okay?"

"Sure, cool. Right then. Get your arse over here then and meet the girls."

I almost run to where Dan has set up the two beds right next to each other, and throw myself onto the right-hand one. Dan goes to move the spunky sock, but I manage to get my hand there first, and I grab hold of it. It's quite wet; he's not lying about the pre-cum. So fucking hot. I'm going to have some fun with that before it goes in the wash, if it ever does.

I turn my attention to Dan. It feels weird being fully dressed, sitting next to a completely naked guy. The fact that he's a total wet dream kind of guy is just the icing on the cake. Fucking hell, this kind of thing doesn't happen to me.

I move my arse across a bit more, so I'm pressed right up against him. My left arm is against his right arm, and I can feel every movement of his muscles as he gently wanks his cock. My leg is right next to his as well, and I adjust its position slightly to make sure there's contact all the way down to where my trainer (his trainer actually) is resting against his right foot. I can't take my eyes off his cock and his legs, but he's talking again, and it jolts me out of my dream world.

"Girls, this is my mate, Tom. This is the one I told you about." For the first time, I drag my eyes off Dan and look at the laptop. Two girls are looking back at me. They're on a bed too, but they're kneeling, and they're only wearing their pants.

The girls wave and say hi. They start to tell me about the fun they're having with Dan, and how they've been waiting for me to get there, but my attention's already drifting back to the fucking horny naked body next to me on the bed. I can't stop staring at him.

Dan sees where I'm looking and nudges me in the ribs. Then he looks back at the screen. "So, girls, you said when my mate got here, you'd lose the rest of those clothes. So how about it? You've seen everything I've got already." He waves his dick at the camera.

The girls giggle and whisper. "Did we say that? Well, maybe soon. But you wouldn't expect us to get naked when your friend is sitting there with all his clothes on, would you?"

I look at Dan, as if needing him to tell me what to do. I don't seem to be able to think or do anything. Sitting rubbing up against Dan's naked body is just too overwhelming. Dan takes control. "Well, get your fucking kit off then, mate. What you waiting for?" I reach down and grab one of Dan's trainers, and take it off. It's the one with the cum on it from earlier, and I sneak a look as I put it on the floor.

But before I can get any further, one of the girls intervenes. "Hold on, boys. That's no fun at all. We want you to undress him, Dan. That'd be much more of a turn-on for us, wouldn't it?" The other girl agrees, and then, as if to back up her point, licks her friend's nipple and giggles again.

They know how to push all of Dan's buttons, that's obvious. "Oh yes. Fucking hot. Do that again!"

"Soon, maybe. You need to take your friend's clothes off first."

"And if I do, what will I get in return?"

There's more whispering at the other end of the webcam link, and Dan turns to me. He leans in close and whispers urgently, "I am *not* touching your dick, and you're *not* touching mine, okay? Whatever the fuck they say, even if they promise they'll fuck each other with a fucking…I don't know…just keep your hands to yourself, right."

The girls have obviously discussed the deal, and one of them is calling Dan, leaning forward toward the camera on all fours with her tits swinging. "Well, if you get your friend nice and naked, we'll do the same to each other. Would you like that?"

Dan's pretty clear that he'd like that, but he protests that it's not enough to offer, if he's going to have to do "fucking queer stuff" like undressing a mate, they've got to do more.

The other girl's head appears from behind her friend, and her hands reach round and start to stroke her tits. "Candy really likes it when I suck her nipples. I'd love to do that to her, but it wouldn't be fair, would it, because your friend isn't ready to join in the fun at all, is he?"

Dan's clearly getting really wound up by the idea of some tit sucking. "Okay, okay, I'll do it." He reaches over and undoes my belt, then the buttons on my jeans. My boxers are in the most disgusting state. They're covered in patches of cum and pre-cum, some drying and some still soaking wet. I suppose there must be some piss there too. I didn't dry my bell-end after Dan pissed on it. I just put it away wet. I wonder how much of this the girls can see. Still, what the fuck?

Dan hesitates at the sight of the boxers nightmare facing him and decides to deal with it later. He kneels up and reaches over to take off my other trainer and my socks. His cock, hard and ramrod straight, is inches from my face, the foreskin pulled back and the end shiny and—Oh fuck, that feels like a bit more pre-cum oozing out to join the toxic mixture already in my pants. Now he pulls at my T-shirt, and I lean forward so it slips easily over my head.

I lift my arse up off the bed, so Dan can slide my jeans off, and he throws them down onto the floor with the rest of my stuff. Another short hesitation, and then he takes hold of my boxers, holding the very bottom of each leg, well away from the danger zone. He pulls them down hard, but my cock gets caught inside the waistband, and as they slide down my legs, my super-erect penis gets pulled right down and snaps back hard against my stomach with a massive slap. It fucking hurts, but it's quite exciting as well, and it starts the pre-cum flowing again.

Dan sits back on his side of our twin bed and stretches out his legs again with the laptop between them. I move back in close and get my body and leg touching his. This time, though, I'm naked too, and my leg rubbing against his is even more fucking arousing, now I'm feeling it directly, and not through my jeans.

Dan's not looking at me, though. His eyes are fixed on the screen. He's talking to the girls and gently rubbing his hand up and down his nob. I have a quick look at the screen, where the girls seem to be doing the tit play that they promised, and then I return my attention to Dan. I start rubbing my own nob, trying to move my hand exactly in time with his as though, somehow, that might connect me with him, allow me to share in his wank, share what's going on in his body and his head.

Dan and the girls have been talking for a while, but I haven't been listening. Suddenly, Dan's talking louder, and I tune in to what he's saying. "You can fucking forget that. There is no way I'm even touching his dick." Whoa. Do they want us to wank each other? Fucking amazing idea!

I look at the screen, where both girls are now naked and sitting propped up on pillows. "But, boys, we thought you might like it if we played with each other a little bit. Don't you want us to?"

"Oh, yeah. Do it please. Do it now." Dan's really getting into this.

"My pussy's very wet, boys. Can you see? Pussy wants to play, but it wouldn't be right unless we all play, would it?"

"Fuck! But you're girls. It's all right for you to play with each other. I'm a guy."

The girls sound very disappointed. I don't know if they're putting it on, but if they are, it's very convincing. I have to give them that. But there's no way Dan's going to give in on this one. He's already made the rules clear more than once, and he's not going to change them that easily.

But then he does. Just like that. "All right. Fuck it. But I'm only doing it for, like, ten seconds, and that's it, right? Tom, shift your fucking hand before I change my mind."

Holy shit! I stop wanking immediately, and move my hand away, so he can get his hand round my shaft and wank me all the way to paradise. My body starts to tingle, and I feel all the hairs standing up on my neck and legs. Dan's hand moves across, and it hovers next to my dick for a second. He takes two enormous breaths, takes hold of my shaft, and looks back at the laptop screen.

"Right then, girls. I hope you get off on this, because I'm never fucking doing it again." His hand starts to move, and my body stiffens with the feeling of lust that sweeps over me. This is the hand he uses on his own nob, and now he's using it on mine. Fuck, it feels amazing. I stretch out my body a bit more, and feel the hairs on our legs rubbing together. This is fucking incredible.

But then he stops. He moves his hand from my dick back to his own. "Okay, girls. I've had my turn. Now it's your go." Fuck. No. That was, like, about two seconds. The bastard. He hardly even started, and it was over. Shit. Shit. Shit!

But, I tell myself, I've already had more stuff happen today than in the rest of my life put together, and I mustn't be greedy. I have to just concentrate on the fucking horny shit that's happening now, and forget about might-have-beens.

I look at Dan, and then back at the screen. The girls are moving round on the bed. They seem ready to push things a bit further. One of them sits between the other one's legs, leans back on her friend, and opens her legs wide. Her friend's hands slide round her body and start moving down over her belly. I'm not very keen to watch what's going to happen next, so I switch my attention back to Dan.

He's really getting into what the girls are doing. He's wanking himself quite hard already, and his arm is rubbing against my body, which I'm loving. I get hold of my own cock and try again to get my wank in rhythm with his.

But again, it doesn't last long. Dan's hand stops moving, and one of girls speaks. "Boys, do you want her to put her fingers inside me?"

Dan's nearly drooling with excitement. "Fuck, yeah. Do it. Please."

"Well. You know, boys, I want her to. But she won't do it. She thinks it wouldn't be fair, because you two boys are not joining in properly."

"What do you mean? Not joining in?" He points his swollen, hard bell-end at the camera, and lets it snap back against his body. "What the fuck do you think this is?"

"But your friend hasn't played with it yet, and we think he should. If you let him have fun with you, we'll do all sorts of things in return. Come on, we can tell he wants to play with it. We can see the way he's been looking at you, Dan."

I look across at Dan. He's looking back at me. It takes him about two seconds to make up his mind. "Right. Do it."

"But, Dan. You said not to touch your—"

"Shut the fuck up, right. I didn't know they were going to finger each other, did I? Go on then. You know you've been fucking gagging for this all day. Get on with it." He settles back against the pillows and fixes his eyes on the girls.

I'm reaching out toward him, when the girl's voice cuts in again, "No, not like that. See how comfortable I am, lying back in my girlfriend's arms, while she plays with my pussy. If you boys were lying like this, it would make me get really horny, and I know I'd cum so much harder. It would turn me on so much to see you lying together like this."

"For fuck's sake. If I do this, I'm telling you, you had better put on a fucking incredible show."

"Dan, I'm so hot already. As soon as I feel my girlfriend's fingers slipping inside me, I think I'm going to cum."

Again, Dan takes about two seconds to make up his mind. I can't believe he's such a pushover. I don't even think the girls are particularly pretty, but I suppose it isn't their faces he's interested in. "Right, mate, get your legs open. I'm coming across." He clambers across the bed, bringing the laptop with him, and kneels between my legs. "Tom, if you fucking cum in my arse crack, you are dead meat, okay? I'm serious."

"Okay, okay. I'll try not to. You'll have to stay still though, or I will. If you start humping about and make me cum, it won't be my fault."

Dan gives me a look that I can't quite work out and then turns round and slides back between my legs, pulling the laptop into place in front of us and adjusting the webcam. Then he leans back, and his body settles against mine, his muscles flexing as he gets more comfortable, and his hard-on sticking straight into the air. I feel his arse cheeks spread around my cock. It feels amazing, but Dan doesn't seem very happy. "Ugh, fucking gross. Do I have to do this?"

The girls, though, seem to be very happy with this new position. The one who does most of the talking looks straight out of the screen at us. "What's the matter, boys? Don't you want to play?"

I open my mouth to speak, but Dan gets in first. "No! It feels fucking disgusting. I've got a bloke's cock in my arse crack. I can't believe I'm fucking doing this."

I think I need to set the record straight. "Well, girls, I'm having a great time, so don't listen to this miserable fucker. I think he'll shut up as soon as you start playing with each other, eh?" The girls giggle, and the one in front turns her head to kiss her friend.

That seems to be enough for Dan. "Fucking get on with it then. And you"—he turns his head toward me for a moment—"you'd better give me the best wank I've ever had, or I'm going to want my money back."

I reach out and close my hand round his shaft. The first touch sends a shiver through my whole body, like an electric shock, and some cum leaks into Dan's arse crack. There's nothing I can do to stop it. I hope he doesn't notice. I start to slowly move my hand up and down.

Because his cock is so near to mine, I expect it to feel the same as wanking myself off, but it doesn't at all. Dan's cock feels really different. I can't quite say why. It's about the same size as mine, but it doesn't feel the same. Mine's got a bit of a bend on it, for a start, and his is dead straight. His foreskin isn't as long as mine either, and it only just covers his bell-end when I pull it right up. Fuck, I could really get into doing this to guys. Why haven't I been doing this all the time, every day? Fucking crazy.

I glance up at the screen. The girl underneath has got her fingers right inside her friend's pussy, and they're starting to make a lot of noise. It sounds like there's going to be some very loud orgasms down that end of the webcam soon, and by the way Dan's body is starting to stiffen up, I think there's going to be one here too. He's stretching out further, with his hands splayed out on the sheets on either side, and his feet flexing and arching. I'm loving the feeling that I'm doing this to him. I'm putting him near to cumming; I'm controlling it. I know it's the girls he's interested in, not me, but it's still my hand that's bringing him close to the edge.

His breathing is quickening now, and I bring my other hand round to grab his ball sack and speed up my wanking hand. I'm making sure that I really work my hand from the very base of his cock, down in the closely trimmed pubes, right up to the tip of his bell. I want to give him the best orgasm I can. He's given me the most exciting day I've ever had, and I want to give him back the only thing that's in my power to give right now.

I suddenly feel things changing. Dan's body stiffens a bit more, and his back arches. His balls seem to draw in toward his body, and his cock gets even bigger and harder. I know what that means, and I get ready to enjoy it with him. I don't want him to waste his cum by shooting it on himself, so I angle his cock a bit to the left, so it's pointing toward my head, shoulder and arm.

With the first shot of cum, he gives a massive grunt; so sexy and hot! His body jerks forward, and then drops back, as the white streams begin to fly from his bell-end. The first one lands on my shoulder, the second on my arm. He keeps pumping and pumping, his body tightening and relaxing, the feelings, the noises and the smells combining into the most incredible sensory overload.

As Dan's orgasm starts to subside, I realize how incredibly close to cumming I am. "Dan, don't move."

"Why?" He's really out of breath.

"If you move at all, I'm going to cum."

"Don't you fucking dare. Think about something gross. I don't know, think about your granny."

I crack up completely. My arms close around him, and just for a moment I hold him close, feeling what it would be like if—

But it's not to be. Dan interrupts my thoughts. "Right. I'm going back to my side of the bed, okay? I'll move slowly!" He starts to lift himself up, and I watch as his arse peels carefully away from my groin and moves away. There's quite a lot of pre-cum on his arse, but he only told me not to actually cum, and I managed not to, so I figure it's okay.

"Girls." Dan's attention is back on the screen immediately. "That was a fucking awesome show. I tell you what, if you want to carry on doing that a bit longer, I'll show you that men can have multiple orgasms too. I could easily manage another one!" Just to demonstrate his willingness, he starts giving his still-hard cock some firm tugs. Then he turns to me. "And you can finish that fucker off yourself, you dirty bastard."

Once again, though, the girls come to my rescue. The one who does all the talking, (Candy, was it?) speaks up. "Shall I tell you what would make *me* cum a second time, Dan? My pussy knows what it wants, and I know it would hardly take anything at all for me to cum. Do you want me to cum? I always cum much harder the second time."

"Fucking stop doing this to me. I just want to watch you and get myself off, and you keep making me do fucking queer stuff. For fuck's sake."

"But, Dan, that's all we want too. You just lie there and play nicely. You're so big and hard, my pussy gets really wet watching you."

"And are you going to finger each other again?"

"Yes. In a minute. We just want one other thing first. Your friend has been really nice to you. We got very hot watching what he was doing to you. Your cum went all over him. We loved seeing that."

"Oh no. Don't even think about it."

"But, Dan, what if I was to do this?" The girl in front turns round on the bed, and checking she's not blocking the view to the camera, starts to lick up her friend's thigh. She's moving up slowly, but it's obvious where she's heading.

Dan's reaction is instantaneous. "Holy fuck! Yes. Keep doing it. Don't stop. Tom, just cum on me, mate. I don't fucking care. Lick her pussy. Fucking do it." His hand starts to fly up and down his nob. He's still completely hard, his bell-end's still wet from the first time, but he's already building for a second one.

I quickly clamber to my knees and face Dan. I want to get close, but I can't block his view of the screen. I think he'd fucking kill me. I kneel with one of his legs in-between mine, and shuffle forward until my knee is right up against his ball sack. I can feel his balls slapping against me as he wanks faster and faster, his eyes glued to the screen.

I kneel up and start wanking. But slowly. I'm so close, and I want to cum at the same time he does. I put my other hand on Dan's thigh, and rub it over the hair. At once, I feel his muscles tense, and his cock thrusts forward. As his orgasm starts, he shouts, "Gonna cum. Fucking do it then." And as the shiny ropes of spunk start to flow, I go over the edge. I feel my whole body go into a kind of spasm, clenching and jerking, shooting and squirting. It's one of those cums that just seems to go on forever, wave after wave of intense, shuddering pulses.

Dan gets the whole load. There's cum right up the side of his face and in his hair, all over his chest and shoulder, and as I look down at my nob, I see a big glob dropping off the end into his pubes.

I'm completely exhausted, and I guess Dan is too. We're both breathing very hard, and I watch his chest rising and falling as I start to come down a bit from my high. Not just the orgasm, but the whole thing, from the moment I came into the room and found him naked and hard.

I flop down on my side, where I can watch Dan as he talks to the girls and then taps at the laptop keys. I don't hear a word he's saying; I just watch him, trying to take in every detail of his body and his softening cock.

He turns toward me. "You enjoy that then?" I grin. "I hate you, you know. You fucking spunked on my face." He runs his finger up his cheek, collecting up some of the white goo that I put there. He looks at his finger for a moment and then wipes it on my chest. Then he leans over his side of the bed, retrieves his other discarded sock, and gives himself a good wipe down with it.

He gets up from the bed and stands looking at me. "You know, when you suggested we should share a room, I should just have said no. You're a fucking animal." I open my mouth to protest, but instead close it again, and just carry on grinning. "Right. I'm going for a shower. I expect you'll want this too." He throws the spunky sock at me, and I let it hit me in the face and fall onto my chest.

I watch him wrap a towel round his waist and pick up his wash things. At the door, he turns, and I see him look down at my crotch, where my nob is still as hard as ever. "Be a good boy while I'm gone."

CHAPTER FIVE

The door clicks shut, and suddenly I'm alone. I check the time. Unbelievable. Just a few hours since that moment in the student union when Dan turned round unexpectedly and knocked me onto my arse.

Fucking hell. It's all happened so quickly. I want to think it all through, go back over it all in my head. Try to make some sense of it.

But maybe not now. Just at the moment, I've got Dan's laptop in front of me, and my cock is hard and demanding that I give it some more attention. I get my hand round it and start giving it a little rub, while I count today's orgasms. Number one, in bed this morning; number two, with the Fleshlight in front of my computer. Those were my last pre-Dan orgasms. That's such a weird thought.

Three was in the toilet when I put Dan's trainer on, and four was in the bar. So that means I've had five so far today. I picture the fifth one again, that thick rope of cum shooting out into Dan's hair and down the side of his face. Fuck, that was so hot!

And on top of that, I've wanked Dan off, and sucked Ryan and made him cum. No wonder I'm feeling super horny then. Time to choose a suitable website, I think, and blow another load.

There's a bleep. I've got a text. I reach down the side of the bed to where Dan threw my jeans and fumble through the pockets for my phone.

It's from Ryan: "yr pic has me rock hard yr so dirty x"

My cock twitches. I think about texting back, but decide to ring instead. Ryan answers on the first ring.

"Hey, Ryan, are you wanking over my pic?"

I hear him laugh. "No. Well, not really. I can't at the moment."

"Oh right, is…" I find I can't remember the name of Ryan's roommate. I'm not sure if Dan ever mentioned it. "Is your roommate in?"

"Yeah, he is."

"Okay. I'd better be careful what I say, then."

"You don't have to. I'm not in the room."

"What?"

"I'm not in the room. I came outside to text you."

"Cool. Where are you now?" There's a bit of a pause. It feels like a slightly embarrassed pause. I try again. "Ryan, what's going on?"

"I'm outside your window."

I almost run over to the window and look out. Ryan is standing on the grass with his phone pressed to his ear. I push the window open, and he looks up as he hears the noise. I end the call and shout down to him, "Ryan, you all right?"

"I needed to get outside. I got really, really horny, and I needed to get out of the room. I just ended up here."

"Great. Look, I'll be down in, like, two minutes. I need to get some clothes on. Wait there." I'm just about to shut the window, but decide instead to give Ryan a quick show. I kneel up on the windowsill and hold onto the curtain rail to steady myself. Looking down, I see Ryan putting his phone away. "Hey, Ryan. Want some of this?" I grab my hard-on with my free hand and start wanking it.

Ryan looks horrified. "Get down, you twat. Someone might see you." He's looking around wildly, to check if anyone is nearby.

I climb down and lean out the window again. "But, Ryan, I thought you'd want to see…" I raise my volume a bit, "My erect penis."

"Fucking shut up will you? You're so embarrassing. If you don't shut up right now, I'm going." He's trying to sound serious, but I can see his smile even from this distance.

"Okay, okay. Hang on. I'll be down in a minute."

I pull the window closed and head for where my clothes are piled in a heap on the floor. I remember the state my boxers were in when Dan took them off and decide to get some clean ones. Just as I reach the wardrobe, a much better idea hits me, and I go round to Dan's side of the beds instead.

His clothes are also in a pile on the floor, and I don't stop even for a moment to wonder if he'll mind me doing this. I pick up his boxers, give them a couple of big sniffs, and put them on. They're tight, white ones, and I take a second to rub my hand over them, feeling how my hard-on fills them and the shape it makes in the stretchy material. Then I get Dan's jeans and slip my legs into them. This is so hot. Next the T-shirt. It's the "Masturbating is not a Crime" T-shirt, and it has some of his smell on it. Part aftershave, part male sweat and masculine fucking. Oh God, I'm loving this.

I look round for socks, but remember that both of his socks got used as cum rags, and they're both on my bed, ready for me to reuse them. I won't bother with socks. The trainers on Dan's side of the bed are mine, of course, and I don't want to wear those. It would be far less exciting. I could just put on the ones I've been wearing for most of the afternoon, but I decide to see what else is in Dan's wardrobe. I find some quite old DCs, which are a bit trashed and fucking hot. I hold one in my hand and can't help myself; I give my crotch a quick rub with it, and have a sniff, breathing in the smells of feet and sweat that have soaked into the leather over the months, maybe years that he's worn them. Fuck. My cock gives a jolt in Dan's jeans, and starts to throb a bit. Fucking hell, this is unreal!

I slip my bare feet into the trainers. Christ, I could just cum right now. "Got to go," I tell myself. "Got to go and meet Ryan." Ryan's downstairs, and he's fit and horny, and he's got a hard-on over a photo of my cock.

As I head out the door and down the corridor, I can feel my cock rubbing on Dan's boxers, my legs rubbing against his jeans, my feet in his trainers. By the time I reach Ryan, I'm insanely horny. When he sees me, he reaches out and moves in for a hug. I almost shout at him, "Ryan, be careful!"

He steps back, with a look of absolute panic in his eyes. "Shit. What? What is it?"

"If you hug me, I think I'll cum."

"What? Is that? I thought there was something wrong…"

"No, it's all right. There's nothing wrong. I'm just so horny, I could blow any second. I'm wearing Dan's clothes, and it's got me really…you know."

There's an immediate change in Ryan. His head and shoulders go down, and he loses all the excitement I'd sensed in him when I first saw him. I hear him sigh. "Look, I think I'd better go."

"What do you mean, go?"

"It was stupid, me coming here. I'll go."

He turns quickly and sets off up the path without looking back. I'm after him in a second. I get ahead of him and grab his shoulders to make him stop. "Ryan, what are you doing? What's the matter?" He won't look at me; he's keeping his eyes down and his body's shaking a bit. I don't know what to do. "Ryan, please talk to me. Did I say something wrong?" Still no response.

I decide to try a yes/no question, see if that's more successful. "Ryan, are you angry with me about something?" He shakes his head and mumbles a "No."

"But you're upset about something?" Another big sigh is all the answer I get, but it's as clear as any words. "Was it something I said? Something about Dan?"

This time Ryan nods his head slowly, and finally, he looks up and fixes me with a bleak stare. "I wasn't thinking. I got so horny looking at your picture. I just wanted to see you, and... but you should go back to Dan. It's not fair, me being here. It's not right."

I move my hands up to his face and brush his hair out of his eyes. I try to choose my words carefully. "Ryan, earlier on, you know, when I sucked you off, and I said I'd come back tomorrow, and you could do whatever you wanted. You remember?" He nods again. "Well, I meant that, you know? I wasn't just saying it. And when I got your text and found you were right outside, I got really excited. And I thought you were too. And now I don't understand what the matter is."

There's a pause, and Ryan opens and closes his mouth a couple of times. I think he's searching for the right words too. "Look. It's all right for you. You say we can, like, fool around and do stuff together, but that's all it is to you, isn't it? It's just a bit of fooling around. You've got a boyfriend, and when you've had a bit of fun with me, you can go back to him, and I'm just fucking...I don't think I can...shit. Shit! Don't you get it? It's not just a laugh for me. I've never done this before. I've never had a boyfriend. I've never even had sex. When you sucked my cock, it was the most amazing thing. It was, like, the best feeling I've ever had, and I want...I want..." His voice trails off, and he starts to sob, his body crumpling and shaking. He looks so small and vulnerable and desperate.

I move forward and draw him close, moving his head onto my shoulder and closing my other arm behind his back. He lets me hold him for a few seconds, and then I feel his arms fold round me and pull me in so tightly that it hurts. He's holding on to me like his life depends on it, and maybe that's how it feels. I smooth his hair and rub his back, and just wait; just let him get everything out of his system. Eventually, he seems to become more peaceful, and the crying stops.

I know I can't let this go on any longer. When Dan came up with the "gay couple" thing, it seemed like a laugh, and it meant I could get to room share with Dan, the thing I wanted most in the world. I knew it might backfire on Dan. I even told him that. But I never thought it would backfire on me. But Ryan's really fucked up about it, and I know I've got to explain things to him. I just don't know how he'll react.

"Ryan, I need to say something, okay? I need to tell you something. You're going to think I'm a real cunt, and you'll probably be really mad at me, but just let me say it, yeah, and then you can tell me to go fuck myself, or you can punch me, or whatever. I don't care. Well…" Christ, I don't know how to say this. "The thing is, er, well, Dan's not actually gay." I wait to see if Ryan is going to respond, but he doesn't. I'm going to have to plow on. "It's, er, we wanted to share a room, because, well, because—FUCK! I can't explain it. It's too complicated. It sounds fucking stupid."

Ryan lifts his head from my shoulder and looks straight at me. "Dan's not gay?"

"No. He says he's completely straight, and I don't know, I think maybe he is. Well, more or less, anyway."

"So why is he going out with you then?"

"He's not. I mean, we're not."

"Not going out?"

"No."

"But what about…weren't you having sex this afternoon?"

"No. We've never had sex; well, not real sex. I've told you, Dan's straight. He just enjoys getting me all fucking horny and desperate. He seems to get off on it. So I've had a couple of wanks over him, that's all. Then, when we went back to the room to watch porn, he was on a video chat with some girls, and they said they'd lick each other out if he'd let me wank him off. So he let me do it. But he was watching the girls the whole time."

"So he's really not gay?"

"No. Well, I don't think so."

"And you're not going out with him?"

"No. I only met him today."

"What? Hang on. Now I'm really fucking confused. Why did you tell me you were going out then?"

Oh shit, here it comes. All I can do is try to keep Ryan from getting too angry, and limit the damage.

"We needed a way to make you change rooms. Dan thought it'd be a laugh, you know, if him and me shared; so we decided to use my room, but when we got there, you'd just arrived, and Dan just said the first thing that came into his head."

"And you made me go and share with that geek?" Oh God. This is going really badly.

"Ryan, I'm sorry. If I'd known you then, I wouldn't have done it. I was so excited about sharing with Dan. You know, seeing him naked and watching him wanking and stuff. I couldn't think about anything else."

There's a long silence, while we stand together, our arms still around each other, with Ryan looking intently at me. I'm not liking the silence, and the longer it goes on, the more I don't like it. I don't know if I should say something, or let go of Ryan, or even just go away completely.

Finally, Ryan seems ready to speak. "So Dan's not gay, although you told me he was. And you're not going out with each other, even though you said you were."

"Yeah, that's right. Sorry. I'm really sorry."

"So are you going out with anyone?"

"No. I've never had a boyfriend. I'm not really out, back home. Not properly."

"But you're telling me all that stuff about wanting to see me tomorrow...you're telling me that's all true."

"Ryan, that's totally true. You've got to believe me."

There's another pause, while Ryan looks hard at me again, and then, "Okay, so can we have tomorrow now?"

"What? Don't you mind about all this? I mean..."

"No, it's all right. Can we start tomorrow early? Like now, I mean?"

"I thought you'd be so mad about it. I thought..."

"Well, I'm not. Not now, anyway. Maybe tomorrow I'll get proper mad about it and come and punch you. But I'm not going to think about it now. Right now, I want to have sex, and I want to have it with you, you cunt."

"Fucking hell. Are you sure?"

"Of course I'm fucking sure. Why? Don't you want to?"

"Yeah, I want to. I want to so much!"

Ryan pulls my head toward him and locks his open mouth onto mine. Our tongues immediately start probing each other's mouths, pushing in and out; our hands move to the back of each other's heads, forcing our mouths together even more tightly. I feel Ryan's crotch starting to rub against mine, and he slips one of his hands into the back pocket of my jeans, pulling me in closer. I move a hand down his back and slip it into his jeans pocket, and press my cock against his. Soon, we're both rock hard again; I can feel his hard-on clearly through the layers of denim, and I know he'll be able to feel mine.

Suddenly, there's a loud wolf whistle from very close by, and we both jump wildly, letting go of each other and stepping back. Two girls go past, whispering and giggling, and disappear into my accommodation block. I try to calm down my breathing and wait for the adrenaline rush to subside. We obviously can't stay here. I have a quick look around. "Come on, let's go down there." I point down the side of the block. "There aren't any windows or lights along there. We can get right out of the way."

"Okay."

I instinctively reach out and take Ryan's hand and set off for the corner of the block at a run, pulling him along with me. We disappear down the side of the building and into the shadows. I pull Ryan round to face me and push him back against the wall, moving back in to kiss him. Immediately, he stiffens, and a momentary panic shows on his face.

In a second, the conversation we had earlier floods back into my head, and I realize what I've done. "Shit, Ryan. I wasn't thinking. I'm really sorry."

"It's all right. I'm okay."

"It's that thing that happened to you; that guy, outside that club?"

"It just—it just came back to me. But I'm okay now."

"Ryan, I'd never do anything that would hurt you. You've got to believe that."

"I do. It was just when you pushed me against the wall. It made me think…"

"Do you want to stop?"

"No. Fuck, no!"

"Do you want to go somewhere else?"

"No. It's okay. I got scared, but I'm all right now." But I can see that he's still breathing hard, and the panicky look hasn't quite gone from his eyes.

"Look, I've got an idea. See what you think of this. You're in charge from now on, and you can tell me to do exactly what you want. I won't do anything unless you tell me to. That way you'll know that nothing bad's going to happen. Okay?"

There's the start of a smile now from Ryan. "Okay. Right." He thinks for a moment, and his breathing slows again as he calms down a bit. "Well, the first thing that's going to happen is…" I feel Ryan's hands on my shoulders, and he swings me round, forcing my back against the wall and pinning me there. "And now the next thing I want is this…" He moves forward squashing me completely against the cold bricks, and, in a moment, his tongue is back in my mouth and his hard-on is rubbing against mine. I just love feeling him taking control like this. I relax and let myself enjoy the waves of excitement and warmth which immediately start to run through my body.

After a while, Ryan stops kissing and grinding against me and smiles again. "Now, what I want you to do is get my cock out." He takes a small step back, so I can get to his flies, and I undo his jeans as quickly as I can. Immediately, his nob jumps up, full and hard; he's not wearing any underwear.

"Ryan. No boxers? You dirty boy."

His smile gets wider. "I took them off. They were a bit messy."

"Cool. I had the same problem with mine." I want to take his dick in my hand, but I have to wait until I'm told. His bell-end is only a couple of inches away from me, and his nob is jolting and jerking in time with this heartbeat, wet with pre-cum. It's all so new and exciting, having a real guy standing there, not just imagining it. The only problem is trying to hold off and not cum too fast. I'm just too horned up. Still, what the fuck?

Ryan starts to move forward, until the tip of his cock touches Dan's jeans, and I watch mesmerized as a bit of pre-cum appears on the denim. I get a sudden jolt like an electric shock. My body shudders with excitement, and a wave of lust runs right through me.

Ryan looks at me. "Now, am I still in charge?"

"Yeah. Completely in charge."

"Okay then. Good."

Ryan reaches out and takes hold of the zip of Dan's jeans, pulling it down and opening up the fly, so he can get his hand inside. I watch as his hand disappears through the hole and I feel him take hold of my balls. I really want him to get my cock out straightaway, but I know I mustn't say anything. He's in charge, and I have to wait until he's ready to do it.

"Are these Dan's jeans then, Tom?"

"Yeah."

"And his boxers as well?"

"Yeah."

"I'm going to make such a fucking mess of them in a minute. I hope he doesn't mind!"

Then, instead of getting my cock out, which was what I thought he'd do, he starts to push his own cock into the open fly of Dan's jeans. I watch it going in, and immediately feel it rubbing against my hard-on, just the thin material of Dan's boxers separating us.

Ryan's face is very close to mine now, and he's breathing hard. "This is so fucking hot. I'm nearly cumming already."

"Do it then."

Ryan throws one hand round my neck, the other round my waist and starts to thrust against me. Then he moves in to kiss me, locking his mouth against mine and pushing his tongue inside. I'm completely squashed against the wall, and Ryan is humping against me, faster and faster, making groaning noises as he kisses me. Suddenly, his orgasm starts. His whole body goes stiff for a moment, then he just lets himself go. He's grunting and moaning as he jerks his hips forward and thrusts his cock against me, squeezing me so hard it hurts. A moment later, I can feel something wet spreading across Dan's boxers. Ryan seems to be getting louder, if anything, even though our mouths are still locked together. Thank fuck we moved down here, out of the way; he's making so much noise.

Eventually, Ryan's body starts to relax, and his breathing slows a little. Neither of us moves for a while, and then he starts to peel his body away from mine. I watch his cock sliding out of my fly, and then Ryan undoes the button and opens up the front of the jeans completely. The inside of Dan's jeans and boxers are covered in spunk, masses of it. I can't resist running the side of my finger over it, wiping up a big glob and lifting it to my mouth. Ryan laughs and rubs a finger over his bell-end, getting it as wet as possible and then transferring it to his own mouth.

Ryan looks down at the shape of my cock in Dan's boxers. "Right, now it's your turn." His fingers start to move over the wet material. "So you ready to cum?"

"You bet. I'm fucking desperate."

"Okay. What do you want me to do?"

"Ryan, you're in charge, remember? You decide."

"Oh, yeah. I'd forgotten that. I'm in charge. Okay, that's cool." But he doesn't do anything straightaway. He seems to still be thinking. "But you're allowed to ask for one thing, if you want. Just one though. Something to make it more exciting. What's it going to be?"

"I want one of your Converse." The words are out before I can stop myself.

"What?"

I've said it now, so there's no point trying to take it back. If Ryan thinks it's disgusting, that's tough shit. "Er, I want one of your Converse. I want to do pervy stuff with it while you're making me cum."

Ryan's eyes widen. "Wow. That sounds proper dirty. Could be hot though. Right, if you want it, you'd better get down there and fetch it."

I kneel between Ryan's legs and take hold of his left ankle, lifting his foot off the ground. I take hold of the sole and slide the hot Converse off his foot. He's wearing a fluorescent green sock. Fucking hell, he's such an emo!

I stand up again, facing Ryan, grinning like a little kid, and holding the Converse. Ryan wraps his hand round my nob, and starts wanking it gently. He looks up at me. "So what you going to do with it then? Just stand and hold it?" He gives my nob a hard squeeze and rubs a bit faster. I lift Ryan's trainer up to my face and put it over my nose and mouth, breathing in hard. Oh God, that smell is such a turn-on; it drives me wild. The hot male smell that comes off a guy's trainers always gets me going, and Converse are even better. The canvas seems to soak up more of that amazing man odor than leather does.

I'm just getting really into it, when I feel the trainer being snatched away from me. Ryan's taking it back and looking into it suspiciously. I think I may have gone a bit too far. "Sorry, Ryan, was that too pervy?"

"No, mate, not pervy enough!" He puts his hand on my chest and pushes me back against the wall. Then he takes his Converse in both hands and slips it over my hard, throbbing cock. I feel the friction as my bell-end rubs against the canvas and slides into the toe end of the shoe. Then he takes hold with both hands, squeezes hard, and starts to wank it up and down my nob, really fast. The feeling's so intense, I can't stop myself shouting out, and I have to grab at Ryan's shoulders to steady myself.

He squeezes the Converse even tighter round my cock and rubs it even faster. It's hurting, but it feels amazing at the same time. I can feel myself about to go over the edge. "Ryan. Oh

God. I'm going to make such a mess in your—oh fuck!" As soon as I've said it, it starts to happen. My arse tightens, my muscles all clench, and the first massive wave of the orgasm breaks over me. My hips jerk forward, and my cock starts shooting, squirt after squirt. It's got to be a big load, when it's this intense, maybe bigger than the one I shot on Dan.

It's almost too intense though, and as my cum starts to subside, I have to put my hand on Ryan's wrist and slow it all down. He lets me get my breath back a little, and then moves in for a kiss, pinning my cock, still wearing its wet Converse, between us.

When the kiss finally ends, Ryan moves back a little and looks down. "Right, I want you to put my shoe back on now."

"Ryan, it's soaking wet. It's going to feel disgusting. I'll try and clean it out, or wipe it, or something."

"Don't you fucking dare. Just put it back on. It's going to be something to remember you by."

I reach down and slide my nob out. It's covered in spunk, and it looks a bit red. I think it might need a bit of TLC with some hand cream later on. I can't risk it getting sore, especially not now. I tip up Ryan's Converse and look inside. Quite a lot of spunk runs down into the heel. It really is very wet in there, and I can't stop myself grinning. I look at Ryan, and he's grinning too.

I kneel down, and Ryan lifts his foot for me to slide the trainer back on. If he thinks it's disgusting, he certainly doesn't show it. As I stand up, he draws me in for another kiss, "Don't think I'm going to take these socks off tonight."

CHAPTER SIX

I suppose it must be morning. The room's flooded with pale light through the drawn curtains, and I'm wrapped up in my duvet, warm and comfortable.

I'm still close enough to sleep for the remnants of dreams to cling round the edges of my mind; dirty, exciting dreams, full of sex and men, and hard cocks. I reach down into the duvet, and take hold of my morning hard-on, giving it a few tugs as I stretch out in the bed and yawn.

Gradually, I begin to piece together where I am, and what's been happening to me. Then I become aware of someone's rhythmic breathing behind me, and suddenly, I remember. When I turn over and face the other way, I'm going to see Dan, asleep in the other bed, right next to mine. The thought gives me a sudden surge of excitement. I'm over on my other side in a matter of seconds and taking in the sight.

He's so close. The beds are still where Dan put them last night for our webcam wank session—right next to each other, almost like being in a double bed with him. Fucking hell, this is so cool!

He's lying on his back, with one arm above his head, on the pillow. I've got a great view of his muscly arm, the hair under his armpit, and the top of his chest. He's so sexy and naked.

My hand goes back instinctively round my cock and starts some slow wanking as I watch Dan's chest rise and fall with his breathing. I wonder if he's completely naked? I hope so.

I really can't remember what happened last night, well, not after about midnight, anyway. I remember coming back to the room after seeing Ryan, and Dan laughing his arse off because I was wearing his clothes. I remember going to the bar, still wearing Dan's things, and getting a bit pissed. Then we went back down to the gardeners' huts and smoked. I can picture us sitting round, passing joints, quite a big group of us, but after that I'm a bit hazy. Hope I didn't do anything stupid.

I focus my attention back to Dan. He's still asleep. He looks so beautiful, lying there; it's like in a film or something. I start to fantasize about burrowing down into his duvet; going down his chest, and into the warm, sweaty darkness; running down over his stomach and into the trail of hair leading to his pubes and his cock.

In my fantasy, he's naked, and rock hard, of course, and I start wondering…maybe I could just sneak a look. If I lifted the duvet very gently and slowly, and just looked underneath for a moment, then I could get a really good wank fantasy going. And it would make the fantasy so much better because it wouldn't just be imaginary, it would be real.

I let go of my cock, free my arm from inside my duvet and reach out, taking hold of Dan's duvet cover down at crotch level. It's so quiet in the room that my own breathing sounds really loud, and I try to hold my breath as I begin to lift the material as slowly and carefully as I can.

Suddenly, there's a loud, insistent noise, and I almost shit myself. My hand jerks back under my covers, and my heart starts beating wildly as I try to work out where I've heard that noise before. Fuck, it's just my phone. Who's texting me at this time of the morning?

Actually, I think I know the answer to that. It's almost certain to be Ryan. I push myself into a sitting position and pull the duvet up far enough to cover my dick. Why am I doing that? I'm surely not embarrassed about Dan seeing my hard-on, not after yesterday, but I suppose old habits die hard. I reach across to where my phone is, in the pocket of my jeans.

It is Ryan: "gon out 2 look 4 james something not right ring me xxx" Shit. What's that all about? Who's James anyway? His roommate, maybe?

Dan's voice cuts into my thoughts. "That Ryan, then?"

"Yeah. It's Ryan."

"You seeing him today?"

I feel myself blush a little. "Yeah, I think so. Maybe."

"You going to fuck him, then?"

"Dan! You can't say that"

"Why not?"

"Because…because you just can't. Ryan is a nice, normal guy. He's not a fucking sex-obsessed pervert like you. It's not right talking about him like that."

"Fair enough. But you *will* fuck him though, won't you? I mean, seriously?"

Oh, what's the point pretending? "God, I fucking hope so. I fancy the arse off him, you know?"

"Yeah, I think I'd guessed that."

The thought of sex with Ryan puts a big grin on my face, and once again my hand slides back under the duvet and round my cock. It's still as hard as ever.

Dan starts sitting up in his bed and watches my hand moving under the covers. "So you having a wank now, or saving it for Ryan?"

I don't need to think about that one. "Having a wank. There'll be plenty left for Ryan as well."

"Okay. You'd better get on with it. Don't think I need one this morning." He starts to slide back down in the bed, as my mouth opens, closes, and opens again. I don't know what to say. Fuck. I just assumed that Dan would need a wank every morning, and that I'd be able to watch, and—

"Fucking hell, tiger. Relax. I'm only joking." With that, Dan takes hold of his duvet and flings it off his body.

He *is* naked, as I'd hoped, and completely hard. Am I ever going to get tired of staring at him? His body looks amazing, the soft light through the curtains making him seem even more tanned and hot and sexy. Oh fuck. This is so great.

Dan's hand moves down and starts to massage his ball sack, and down between his legs. He looks hard at his nob, inspecting it. "Got any lube or anything? Don't want it to get sore, do we? Had a lot of action yesterday."

"Yeah. I'll get it." I throw back my own duvet, and the excitement of being naked and hard in front of Dan hits me with a shudder. I look across at Dan, and he's laughing at me. I'm not sure why. I look down. Is something wrong with my body, or my cock? But no, it isn't that. It's my feet. I'm wearing two white sports socks, and Dan recognizes them. They're the ones he used to wipe up his cum last night. It's funny, I don't remember putting them on. It must have been when I was a bit fucked after all that weed.

I fleetingly wonder if I should be embarrassed. Some people might think it's a bit weird wearing socks that another guy has just spunked on. But fuck it; I'm not embarrassed. I don't need to be. The dirtier I am, the more Dan seems to like it. I lift one of my feet up and bend my leg round so I can look at the sock. It's dry, but the stains show up clearly. I lean forward so I can get my head right down for a closer inspection. "Mmmm, cummy."

Dan snorts with laughter. "You dirty animal. Fucking stop it, will you? Get me that lube, now, or I'll go and do it in the fucking shower instead."

"Okay. Okay." I'm across the room in a moment and unzipping the bag where I keep the things I wouldn't want my mum to see. I find the lube, but, of course, that isn't the only thing in the bag. There's my Fleshlight as well. Yes, brilliant idea! I wonder if Dan has ever tried one? I wonder if he'll want to? Only one way to find out. "Dan, ever used one of these?" I hold up the tube for him to see.

He looks across. "Oh cool, a Fleshlight. No, but I've always wanted to have a go with one. Is it as good as people say?"

"Fucking amazing. Seriously. Want to try it out now?"

"Yeah." Dan slides forward and sits on the end of the bed, with his cock bouncing around. "What do I do? Just stick it on my nob and rub it up and down?"

"Well, you can do, but…" I have a sudden flashback to the two girls on the webcam, and how they talked Dan into doing all sorts of things he wasn't planning to do. "But that doesn't sound like much fun at all."

Dan picks up the reference to the girls straightaway. "Don't you fucking start that! I had enough of that last night. 'It'd be more fun if you did this, Dan. It'd be more fun if you did that.' That ended with you fucking cumming on my face, you cunt."

"But it *was* more fun. You've got to admit that. I fucking loved it."

Dan smiles that hot smile. "I'm not fucking admitting anything. Anyway, what disgusting queer shit have you got in mind this time?" Then he adds quickly, "I'm not saying I'll do it, but, well, go on then."

I move across a little closer so I'm kneeling on the floor almost between Dan's legs, with the Fleshlight in one hand and a tube of lube in the other. "Well, it *is* good if you just, like, stick it on and wank with it, but it's much better if you fuck it. What I like to do is, well, I stick it into one of my trainers—"

"I should have guessed, you pervert."

"No, hold on. It's not a pervy thing. Well, all right, it is a little bit. But it's what loads of guys do. You don't need to have a thing about trainers, or feet, or anything. You stick it in a shoe, put it on the bed, put a pillow on top, and then you can lie on top and fuck it. You can fuck it as hard as you like. It almost feels like having a real fuck."

As soon as I've said it, I look across at Dan, and I know my face has given me away. It's so fucking obvious that I've never had a real fuck, and I'm just spouting stuff I've read on the Internet.

Dan looks back at me for a second, but he doesn't give me a hard time over it. "Sounds cool. I'll let you set it up for me. I suppose you'll want one of my trainers, won't you, you dirty little bastard?"

"Well, that'd be really hot." Suddenly, another thought hits me. "Hang on, though, I've got a better idea."

"Oh shit."

"But it would be much more fun."

"You can fuck off."

"Dan, listen. Look, I just thought that seeing as there's two of us, we could hold it for each other. I'll hold it for you while you fuck it, and then…" I look up at him, trying work out how he's reacting to this. "And then you hold it for me."

"I should have known you'd come up with something like this. Fucking hell."

"You could close your eyes and imagine I'm a girl."

"Oh yeah? Like that'd work. Why would I be shagging a girl with a dick and hairy legs?"

"You won't feel my dick. I'll hold the Fleshlight so my dick's underneath it. If you close your eyes, you'll just get into it and forget it's not a girl."

"It's just another excuse for you to feel me up. I said no touching, remember? Not that you've taken any fucking notice of that so far."

"I won't feel you up. I'll be holding this with both hands." I hold up the plastic tube, and move it into position between my legs.

"I must be fucking insane." Yes. He's going to do it. "But I'm going first. I'm not sticking my dick in it after you've spermed in it. Is it clean?"

"Yes, it's clean. I always wash it out, after."

"Good. Come on, then. Give us that lube. How much do I need?"

"Can I do it?"

"What? Don't you ever stop?"

"No. I want to do it. Please. Anyway, you don't know how much to use, you said."

"All right. Get on with it then. But ten seconds max, okay? I'm timing you. And don't get fucking overexcited."

"Okay, I promise." I hold the plastic tube in place between my thighs and squeeze a big dollop of lube onto my fingers. Dan watches as I move my hand toward the hole in the Fleshlight.

"Ugh, fuck. It's an arsehole. That's gross!"

I bury my sticky fingers deep inside the hole and start to move them round. "Well, what did you expect? I'm not going to have one that looks like a pussy, am I? You won't be able to see it once you get going, anyway."

I collect a bit more lube and spread it over both my hands. Then I reach out to Dan's cock and rub first one hand, and then the other right down the length of his shaft. He stiffens, and his cock jolts in my hand. "Aah, you fucker."

I make the most of my ten seconds, and massage the lube into every millimeter of Dan's hot and very hard cock. In the end, Dan reaches out and takes hold of my wrists. "Okay, that'll do. You're starting to enjoy that too much. Come on, then."

I wipe the excess lube onto my own nob and get up, moving round to the bed and climbing on. I get myself arranged on my back and look up at Dan, who's now standing facing me at the end of the bed. I can't stop myself. "Dan, my pussy is so wet for you. I want you to fuck me so hard."

"Shut the fuck up! How am I supposed to do anything when you're taking the piss?"

"Sorry. Come on, then."

Dan moves forward and kneels between my legs. I sit myself up a bit, so I can see what I'm doing, and get the Fleshlight in position. With one hand I hold the clear plastic tube, with the other, Dan's nob. I push the tube down and watch as first the bell-end and then the shaft start to slide inside. I'm so pleased I got the see-through one. I can see everything that's going on inside, and it's so fucking hot.

Dan shuffles forward a bit more, and starts to lower himself down, with his elbows on either side of me. Then I feel his legs moving apart, sliding across mine, the hair on his legs rubbing against my skin and setting off a wild excitement which runs right up through my body. I close my legs a little and adjust my grip on the Fleshlight.

Dan's hips move back, and I feel the muscles in his body tighten and flex as he pushes forward. The first push is quite slow and careful, but he soon picks up the pace and starts thrusting, still on his elbows, keeping his chest a little bit clear of mine.

It's not long before he's starting to make some noise, just quiet grunts and gasps, but enough to show me he's liking it. I look up at him, moving backward and forward as he pushes in and out of the Fleshlight, a look of complete concentration on his face, and his eyes tightly closed.

"Dan. How's it feel?"

"Shut the fuck up."

"Sorry."

He's really starting to pick up the pace now; his thrusts are getting stronger, and I'm having to hold really tight to stop him forcing the Fleshlight out of my hands. I'm holding the tube right against my own dick, so that every thrust from Dan makes it slide against my hard-on. Dan's legs are rubbing against mine. I can feel the hair on his thighs and his ball sack, which adds another layer to the sensory overload I'm experiencing. He's breathing a lot harder now and making loads of noise, his face close to mine.

I can't believe how hot this is. I'm so close to cumming.

No. Mustn't cum yet. Got to hold off a bit longer. I try to lift the Fleshlight slightly, so it isn't rubbing against my nob, and I concentrate all my thoughts on holding it still, while Dan's fucking gets even harder and faster.

I wish I knew what he was imagining. It's getting him so worked up, whatever it is. I wish there was just a bit of room for me in his fantasy, just somewhere on the edge of his thoughts, but I know that's not going to happen.

But fuck it. I don't care. I've got the hottest, horniest, sexiest guy lying on top of me, thrusting and fucking, building up to an orgasm. So what if he isn't thinking about me; this is fucking amazing!

Until now, Dan's been leaning on his elbows, with his hands on the bed on either side of me. Now, suddenly, he takes hold of my shoulders, gripping them hard, and I feel the thrusting get even more wild and intense. He's nearly there.

Dan's eyes open, and he stares straight at me. "Fucking hold tight." And then he starts to cum, each squirt accompanied by a juddering thrust and a deep, full-voiced shout. Five, six, seven huge thrusts, before it starts to subside, but still moving in and out, the silky skin of the Fleshlight stimulating every one of his nerve endings and keeping the orgasm going on and on.

Eventually, Dan's hips stop moving, and he lets his body fall on top of mine. I can feel him gasping for breath, his chest moving against mine, his head against my shoulder. "Fucking hell, this thing is amazing. I've got to get one." A few more deep breaths, and then, "Right, it's your go. Turn over."

Without lifting himself off me, he leans across to the left and rolls me over on top of him.

I lever up the top half of my body and look down to where Dan's cock, still hard, is buried right inside the clear plastic tube. Dan's hands move down from my shoulders, take hold of the Fleshlight, and pull it up and away, freeing his cock. He moves it straight across to mine, and slides it on. I gasp with the intensity of the feeling, and Dan grins. "I've lubed it up for you, see?" And I know that my cock is sliding into Dan's cum, I'm fucking in Dan's cum, and the sheer, animal lust that produces sends me into a frenzy. I start fucking the Fleshlight so hard that I wonder if I'm going to break it.

My hips are grinding my cock over and over again into the hot, wet tube, my hands holding tighter and tighter to Dan's shoulders, and my breathing turning to gasps. This is going to be the quickest Fleshlight cum I've ever had, but there's no point trying to hold it back. There's no way I can hold it back. And I don't want to. I want to give in to it, to let it take me over and engulf me.

And then it does. I bury my face in Dan's neck and feel the orgasm start. I'm hardly aware of the thrusting, jerking, and grunting I'm doing; all I know is the huge, overwhelming feeling of the orgasm. It's like I can feel it in every cell in my body, so intense, so overwhelming, so hot!

I keep thrusting until every last drop of cum has squeezed out into the Fleshlight, and every last bit of feeling has subsided, and then I let myself collapse onto Dan. He's still breathing quite hard from his own orgasm, and I'm completely out of breath. I lie there for a while, feeling our chests moving against each other. I know this isn't going to last for much longer, so I want to enjoy it while I can. Soon, Dan stirs. "Are you going to get off me, or what? I'm getting a cramp in my fucking hand." He might know how to get me wildly turned on, but he sure as fuck knows how to break the mood as well.

I clamber up and kneel back on Dan's legs, taking the Fleshlight from him, with my nob still inside it. Dan looks up at me. "If you fuck Ryan that hard, you'll snap him. He's only a skinny little fucker."

"Dan, shut up! You can't say that about Ryan. It's wrong. I'm not going to fuck him, anyway. We're going to make love."

Dan's laughter explodes, and his body jerks up from the bed. "We're going to make lurve." I really want to be angry with him, but I can't do it, and now I'm laughing too. It takes both of us over. I'm trying to hold the laughter in. Dan's wiping his eyes with the back of his hand.

Eventually, Dan slaps my leg. "Come on, then, tiger. Move. I need to get up. If I don't get to the bog, I'm going to piss myself." I move my leg so that he can get up, and turn round on the bed so I can watch him as he finds a towel and collects the things he needs for his shower, still laughing to himself.

At the door, he turns back to face me, grinning. "Tom, mate, that thing's awesome. I fucking love it." He looks at the Fleshlight, with my half hard nob still inside. "And don't do anything dirty with all that cum, will you?"

Now, there's an idea…

CHAPTER SEVEN

Today started so well, and now it's all gone a bit shit. All the excitement with the Fleshlight seems ages ago, though it can't be more than an hour or two.

Ryan and I are walking up a muddy footpath in the rain, getting colder and wetter by the minute. It wasn't actually raining when we came out, but it's making up for that now. It's fucking pouring down. All my clothes are soaked through, clinging to my body, and my feet are squelching in my trainers. If this is a joke, I'm not going to be happy.

Ahead of me, Ryan stops and turns. "What do you think? Give up?"

"Ring him again. If he doesn't answer this time, we'll give up, okay? If we stay out in this, we'll get fucking pneumonia or something."

Ryan finds the number, and I hear it ringing. No answer. Ryan bites his lip. "Let's go back and get dry. If he still hasn't turned up then, I'll come out again."

I look at him, his hair plastered down against his face, the water dripping down onto his already soaked T-shirt, and the worried look in his eyes. "Ryan, you're such a nice guy. You know that? You don't have to do this. You don't owe him anything, do you?"

Ryan shrugs and manages a faint smile. I move toward him and put my arms round his waist. "Can I kiss you? Before we go back inside? I really want to." Ryan puts his hands round my shoulders and moves his head toward mine. As our mouths lock together, and I feel his tongue moving against mine, all thoughts of the weather recede for a few seconds.

Then we set off, back toward the uni buildings. Ryan takes my hand, and we huddle together and lean forward against the driving rain.

I think back to Ryan's text, first thing this morning, and to the call I'd made after I'd washed out the Fleshlight and put it away.

"gon out 2 look 4 james," Ryan had put in his text, "something not right." It turned out that James *was* Ryan's roommate, as I'd thought, the geeky, mardy one. They'd had a long talk last night, with James moaning about life, the universe, and everything. Ryan had gone to the toilet, and when he'd got back, James wasn't there. He still wasn't there this morning, and Ryan was getting worried.

Hence our morning walk, wandering about aimlessly in the hopes of stumbling across him. I hadn't minded too much until it started tipping down with rain; then I went off the idea big time. And, of course, we hadn't found him.

Still, we're on our way back now, and I'm holding hands with Ryan, and things are looking up. Very soon now, we'll be able to get out of our wet clothes and warm up. The thought of Ryan taking off his clothes gets an immediate reaction from my nob. It's only a twitch, but I love it when that happens.

As we come round the corner of the accommodation block, there are some lads smoking under the porch, right outside the front door. I instinctively try to pull my hand away, but Ryan's having none of it. "Don't you want to do this?" I've never held hands with a guy in public before. I don't suppose Ryan has either. Thinking about it, I haven't held hands with a guy *ever* before, but, fuck it; it's too late to bottle out now. A couple of the lads are watching us out of the corner of their eyes as we go past. Neither of them says anything, but I can tell they're looking. My cock gives another twitch, and I turn to Ryan and smile. He grins back at me. "Well, I guess that's our cover blown."

Ryan puts his key into the door, and we peer inside. No one there. I start to wander round the room. "What do you think's going on? What did he say exactly, before he went?"

"Well, nothing really. I was getting a bit fed up of him, to be honest, so I'd stopped listening a bit. He was just ranting on about stuff. His school, everyone who went to his school, his parents, his sister. Everyone and everything—except him, obviously. It was all someone else's fault."

"And then he just disappeared?"

"Yeah."

"Well, he's not here now, and I'm freezing to death. I'm going to hit the shower and warm up."

"Do you think we should tell someone, though? I mean, he's not the kind of person you'd think would stay out all night, is he?"

"Suppose not."

"I've got a bad feeling about it."

"Okay. Look, why don't we ask Dan what he thinks? See if he's got any ideas?"

"Worth a try."

We set off straightaway for the walk back to my room. Ryan takes my hand again. I'm gritting my teeth a bit as we walk down the stairs, but the smokers have gone back inside, and we don't see anyone all the way there. We're so wet that the walk doesn't seem to make us any wetter. When I open the door, Dan is sitting on the bed, wrapped in a towel, with the laptop on his knees. He looks up as we come into the room, shivering, and with water dripping onto the floor around our feet.

"Christ, lads. You didn't have to go and fuck out in the rain. You could have done it in here."

Once again, I get that mixture of excitement and embarrassment that I got when Dan started talking about sex in front of Ryan before. "Dan! Shut up. We haven't been fucking."

"Why not?"

"What? Because, well, we...look, you can't say that. Sorry, Ryan."

But Dan's just getting going. "Hey, Ryan. Tom fancies the arse off you, you know. He told me this morning."

"Fucking hell, Dan. Shut up, please!" I can feel redness starting to spread up my neck and into my face.

"So I thought you'd been in the woods or somewhere, you know, getting stuck in. He does want to fuck you, Ryan, mate, he told me that too, so I hope you're up for that."

Oh shit. Now he's really gone too far. "Ryan, look, I didn't really say. Well, I may have sort of...I mean...I..."

Suddenly, I feel Ryan's arm slide round my waist. "Well, I was kind of hoping."

"What?"

"I mean, if you want to." He seems to be struggling for words.

Dan's ready to help out. "Fuck me in the ass. I think that's the phrase you're looking for."

"Yeah. If you want to fuck, to fuck me, well, I want that too."

"Ryan, of course that's what I want." My cock certainly seems to agree. It goes from twitchy to rock hard in about five seconds. "Are you sure, though? You know, after what happened."

"Yeah, I'm sure. But not now though. I'm too fucking cold."

"Right. We need to get showers. And we came over to tell Dan about James."

Ryan suddenly looks serious again. "Oh yeah. Shit, I'd forgotten."

I turn to Dan. "Dan, you know James. The guy you were sharing with, the geeky one? Well, he's disappeared."

Dan looks suitably confused. "What do you mean, disappeared?"

"Well, Ryan was talking to him last night—"

But Dan doesn't let me get any further before he interrupts. "Look guys, why don't you go and get your shower? I think that's more important right now, don't you? You can tell me about geek boy later."

"Oh, okay."

"And make sure you clean up the shower after you've finished. I might have to use it after you."

It takes me a few seconds to work out what he means. "You mean go in the shower together? Fuck, yeah. That'd be so hot."

Dan laughs. "Of course you go in the shower together, you twat. What were you planning on doing?"

"I don't know. I hadn't thought about it. I suppose I just thought...Fuck. That'll be so dirty, being in the shower together." Ryan and I are both grinning all over our faces.

"Well, get going then. For fuck's sake, you're like a couple of little kids."

I grab at my T-shirt and pull it up over my head, unsticking the wet material from my skin, and stepping out of my trainers at the same time. I'm fucking loving this. Getting naked in front of Dan and Ryan at the same time. Fucking hell! Ryan moves closer to me and pulls my head toward his to whisper, "Tom, I've got a boner."

I put on a loud stage whisper in return, "It's okay. Dan won't mind. He loves looking at cock; the harder it is, the more it turns him on." I look back to the bed, where Dan is sitting watching us. He gives us a small smile, the really sexy smile that turns me on so much, and then sticks both of his middle fingers up. Then he goes back to whatever he's doing on his laptop.

I look back at Ryan, give him a grin, and start to take off my jeans. By the time I'm sliding my wet boxers down my legs, my cock's so hard it's throbbing. Seeing it bouncing around as I take off my socks seems to relax Ryan, and he strips the rest of his clothes off as quickly as he can. God, his body is so sexy. And so different from Dan's; skinnier, and tighter somehow.

I search around, but I can only find two towels, a big one, which I give to Ryan, and a small one, which I stretch round myself. It's so tight, there's absolutely no doubt what's going on underneath, but if we see anyone in the corridor, I guess I can cover it up with the shampoo bottle. We set off for the door, but then a thought strikes me; it's a bit of an awkward one. "Ryan, you weren't expecting to…I mean, in the shower…do you want me to, well…"

Once again, the voice from the bed chips in, "Fuck you in the ass. I think that's what you're trying to say."

"Dan, shut the fuck up."

"Just trying to be helpful."

"Well, don't." I turn back to Ryan. "I mean, I didn't know if…well, we haven't tried…shit!"

"Oh, for fuck's sake." Dan to the rescue again. "Do I have to sort everything out for you? Look, you go and have some nice, hot fun in the shower; no penetration needed. I'm going out to rugby practice in a bit. I need to grapple some real men. You queers are doing my fucking head in. So you can come back here later and fuck his brains out."

Yet again, I just don't know what to say. He's sitting there on the bed, all sexy and cute, and looking so pleased with himself. I just let my mouth open and then close again.

It's Ryan who speaks instead. "Sounds great to me. Come on, then." He reaches for my hand and leads me out the door.

As we head down the corridor, I decide to check that Ryan's okay with all this. "Ryan, do you really not mind when Dan says stuff like that?"

"Mind? I fucking love it!"

I'm grinning again. "Cool. And are you sure about, you know, fucking?"

"Totally sure."

"Aren't you worried about it hurting, though?"

"Well, a bit. I know how big your nob is, remember? But it will be fine. I've been practicing." He gives me a sly smile.

"Practicing? What do you mean?"

"I started with the handle of a hairbrush I nicked off my mum. Then when I had my eighteenth birthday, I went to the sex shop and bought a dildo."

"Wow, seriously? I've never dared go in one of those places."

"It was actually okay. A woman came over and asked me what I was looking for. I nearly ran out the door, but I made myself stay. We had this surreal conversation about dildos and butt plugs."

"And you practice with it?"

"Yeah. I fucking love it. Wanking with that thing up my arse is so intense. It'll be even better when it's your cock, though."

When we get to the shower, there's someone in there. I look at Ryan. "Shall we go upstairs, try the one on the next floor?"

"Yeah, we could."

At that moment, though, I hear the bolt sliding back, and the door to the shower opens. A load of steam comes out, followed by a rather nice, big, muscly guy, wrapped in a towel. I wonder if he's one of the rugby lads that Dan's going to be grappling with. I certainly wouldn't mind grappling with him, that's for sure. He gives us an odd look as he goes past. "All right, lads?"

"Yeah, mate. You?" I wonder what he's thinking, as I watch him disappear down the corridor. I can't help imagining him at rugby practice, telling the other lads about the queers he saw going into the shower together. What would Dan say to that?

It's very warm and steamy inside the shower already. I wonder if rugby lad had a wank in here. I hope so. He must have been in here a while, to have got the place this steamy.

Ryan leans into the cubicle and turns the water on. We take off our towels and hang them up, and then step into the shower and pull the door closed behind us. Immediately, Ryan's hands are all over me, and he pulls me in toward him and locks his mouth against mine.

For a long time, we just stand together, enjoying exploring each other's bodies with our hands, and each other's mouths with our tongues, our two cocks pressed side-by-side between us, and the reviving feeling of the hot water running over us.

Eventually, Ryan breaks free, and reaches up to unclip the showerhead from the rail. "I'm glad the showers aren't fixed to the wall. It's much more fun if you can do this with it." He points the showerhead at my chest and starts to move it slowly down my body. When the jet of water hits my bell-end, the feeling is so powerful, it makes me gasp, and my body stiffens.

Ryan moves the jet slowly down the shaft of my cock and onto my balls. I tense up even more, letting out another shout, and grabbing hold of Ryan's shoulders to steady myself.

Then he kneels in front of me, keeping the jet of water firing against my ball sack, and takes my cock in his other hand. He looks up at me, gives me a little grin, and I watch as my cock begins to slide into his mouth. It feels amazing, so intense. I lean back against the wall of the cubicle, and let my hands rest on Ryan's head, running through his hair, as he starts to suck my cock. "Oh God, Ryan, keep doing that!"

He does. The mixture of feelings—from his mouth and tongue on my cock, and the water on my balls—is driving me wild. I grab hold of Ryan's head, and stop him sucking, I'm so close to cumming, and I want to make this last, at least a bit. When it feels safe, I relax my grip on his head a bit, and he starts moving on my cock again, but slower. Even so, I keep getting right to the edge of an orgasm and having to pull out to calm down a bit.

Then Ryan sits back on his heels and starts to move the showerhead, firing the jet of water up and down my shaft again. "Ryan, that's so intense. Fucking hell."

He looks up at me. "Cum in my mouth. I really want you to. Fuck my mouth!"

Before I have time to say anything, the jet of water is back on my balls, and my bell-end is disappearing again into Ryan's mouth. But he doesn't go down on my cock this time; he's waiting for me to take over. I put my hands on either side of his head and take hold, and then tense my hips and thrust them forward. Ryan's free hand comes up, and his thumb and finger close round the base of my cock. I pull back and thrust in again.

"Ryan, is that all right? I don't want to hurt you." The only answer I get is that Ryan's hand grabs the shaft of my cock even tighter and pushes me further into his mouth. It's all the answer I need. I'm so close to cumming that I'm desperate for it. As I start thrusting, I can feel the orgasm building up, deep inside me. I tighten my muscles a bit more and concentrate all my attention on watching my cock sliding in and out of Ryan's mouth. I'm panting already and can hear myself getting noisier and noisier. If there's anyone walking past, they're bound to hear me. Fuck it, I'm going to cum.

The orgasm takes me over completely, the feelings and the moment are everything, just holding on to Ryan's head and pumping squirt after squirt of jizz into his mouth. Nothing else matters; nothing else exists at all for those few seconds.

Eventually, the orgasm starts to subside, and I let myself collapse back against the wall of the shower cubicle. Ryan takes my dick out of his mouth and pumps it a few times with his hand, milking the last few drops of cum and licking them off with his tongue. Then he stands up, and we move our mouths together for another kiss. For some reason, I can picture my sperm swimming around inside our mouths, washed backward and forward between us in the saliva, and it's such a hot thought. God, I think of some fucking weird things!

When the kiss finishes, I look at Ryan and smile. "Want me to do the same thing to you?"

"Well, I would like that, but there's something I'd like more." He hesitates.

"Go on then."

"Right. There's something I do in the shower, sometimes. I want you to do it to me now. It's proper dirty though."

"I don't care. Just tell me what you want, and I'll do it."

"Okay." Ryan still has hold of the showerhead, and he lifts it up to look more closely at it. He begins to rotate the circular plate where the water comes out, and the jet changes, making a wider spray. "No. Wrong way." He turns it back in the opposite direction, and the soft sprinkle of water turns into a hard, narrow jet, fierce and concentrated. I move my hand in front of the jet and feel how powerful it is.

"Ryan? You want me to point this at your cock? It'll fucking kill."

"No. I want it on my hole."

"Your arsehole? Seriously?"

"Yeah. It feels fucking amazing. And if you're doing it to me, it's going to be even better."

"Cool. Let's do it."

Ryan gives me a big grin and starts to sit on the floor of the shower. "You know, Tom, I never thought I'd ever tell anyone about doing this kind of dirty shit. But it's easy telling you about it. Don't know why."

"No? But that's good, though. Anyway, you know loads of dirty stuff about me, so it kind of evens things up."

"Suppose so. Come on, then. Kneel down here." He points between his legs, and I lower myself down. Ryan hands the shower to me and adjusts himself so his legs are in the air on either side of my head and his arse between my knees. I move his ankles onto my shoulders and run my hand over his leg and foot. So hot.

"Right. Here goes." I take a firm hold on the showerhead and move the jet of water down Ryan's leg, slowly and smoothly, toward his arse. I don't want to hit his actual hole just yet, so I keep it just a couple of inches away and circle it round. I hear Ryan draw in his breath, and I feel the muscles in his legs tighten. He takes hold of his cock and starts pumping it, and I circle the spray of water, moving it closer and closer, until it shoots right onto his tight little arsehole. Ryan jerks and gasps. "Oh fuck! That's amazing. Keep it there."

I keep watching Ryan's hole to make sure that the water is hitting the exact spot and feel up his leg with my free hand. I cup his foot for a few seconds and then move it across toward my mouth. I start licking, right the way up his foot, from the heel, and he instinctively curls and flexes his toes. I stick his big toe in my mouth and start to suck on it, running my tongue round it and then biting down gently on it.

In the jet of water, I can just see Ryan's arsehole open and close as it responds to the super-hard massaging of the water. He's really panting and moaning now, and I can tell he's going to cum soon. I reach down with my free hand and move his hand off his cock, so I can take over. I wrap my hand round the shaft—it's *so* hard—and start to wank him. It only takes a few more seconds before I feel his body tense up even more, and his grunts become deeper and louder. I try to wank him a bit faster, without moving the place where the jet of water is hitting.

The first shot of cum flies high into the air and lands on his chest; the second and third reach his face, and he just goes on and on, shooting and shooting. In the end, I feel him easing off a bit, and I slow down my wanking hand. Then I let go of his cock and twist the top of the showerhead round to make a less powerful stream of water. Ryan seems happy to just lie there, and let me play the water round his arsehole and up over his balls and cock, as he begins to come down from the orgasm.

"Ryan, you shot so much cum. I can't believe it. If I didn't know better, I'd think you'd been saving it up."

"That's how it felt. It felt like I'd been saving it up all my life, waiting for you to come and do that to me."

"Oh, Ryan. I think that's the nicest thing anyone's ever said to me. Shit. Don't go saying stuff like that. You'll get me all choked up."

Ryan reaches out and pulls my head down to his and kisses me. "Okay, I won't say anything else. Can we wash each other now? I'd really like that. And then we can go back to your room, and well…Dan says you've got to fuck me in the ass."

I laugh. "Dan says I've got to fuck your brains out."

"You'd better do it then. Wouldn't want to let Dan down, would we?"

CHAPTER EIGHT

It takes ages before we're ready to come out of the shower. We just can't leave each other alone—hugs, kisses, more hugs—and in between, we manage to get each other washed. The feel of Ryan's mouth and body pressed against mine and the steaming hot water running over us—I just want to stay in there forever.

Eventually, Ryan reaches over and turns the water off, and we step out and find the towels. We're both hard again. Actually, neither of us really got soft after we spunked up in the shower. The whole thing was too exciting, and I was thinking about what was going to happen when we got back to the room. I think Ryan was too.

He's certainly thinking about it now. He's drying me between my legs and rubbing the towel over my cock and balls. "So do you really think that thing's going to fit inside me?"

I hope he's not worrying about it. "Do you still want to... you know?"

"Are you joking? I can't wait!"

Thank God for that. At last, I think it's actually going to happen. Happen to me. Real sex. Not just imagining it. Fucking hell, I'm so excited. I can't stop myself grabbing Ryan and giving him another big snog before we wrap the towels round ourselves and get ready to leave. Ryan's got the big towel, so he's okay. Mine's seriously too small, and I have to adjust it a couple of times to try to make my hard-on less obvious.

As we open the door onto the corridor, there's someone going past. Fuck. There would be. He looks at us, and his eyebrows go up, but he doesn't say anything. Ryan grins at me and then shouts after the guy, "Save water, mate. Shower with a friend," but the guy just keeps walking.

We're soon back at the room, and as we go in, I'm a bit surprised to find Dan's still there, sitting on the bed in his rugby kit, with the laptop on his legs. He looks up straightaway and gives us a dirty grin. "Nice shower, boys?"

"Amazing," says Ryan.

"So." I don't feel like being subtle just at the moment. I'm too horny. "Aren't you going to fuck off to rugby, then?"

"Yeah. Not for a bit, though. About half an hour. Why, are you—Oh fucking hell." He's looking at the bulge in my towel. "Are you hard again, you animal? For fuck's sake. Okay, I'll get out of here." He starts to get up off the bed.

"It's not just me, you know. He's almost as bad." I reach across and grab at Ryan's dick through the towel.

Ryan knocks my hand away, but he's smiling. He looks at Dan. "You don't have to go just because…I mean, we can wait."

"Doesn't fucking look like it."

"Or we can go back to my room. That'd be easier."

"Look, I don't mind fucking off now, so you can, you know, make sweet *lurve*."

I'm just about to tell Dan to shut up, but Ryan gets in first. "No, it's okay. We'll make *lurve* back at mine. Expect you can find some nice things to do on that laptop while you're waiting for rugby to start. By the way, that rugby kit is fucking sexy, you know."

Shit. I can't believe Ryan just said that. He seems so much more confident, all of a sudden. I really don't think he would have said something like that to Dan yesterday. Dan, of course, loves the compliment. "Yeah? So am I turning you on too, you dirty little cunt? Think I should be in one of those nude calendars with a rugby ball in front of my bollocks?"

Ryan grins. "I'd buy it."

"Be a waste of money with you two, though. You'd have stuck all the fucking pages together by the second of January."

I stick my middle finger up at Dan in a halfhearted way, as my mind is already moving on to the things we'll need to take with us to Ryan's room. I'm hoping this won't turn out to be a mistake. If we get there and James has come back, I'll be pretty pissed off, but I don't suppose that's very likely now.

I move over to where Ryan and I dropped our clothes in a big pile when we were getting ready for our shower, and then remember that they're soaking wet.

"Shit. We can't wear these." I turn to Ryan. "Do you want to wear some of my clothes?"

He gives me a big grin. "Can I choose?"

"Yeah, of course." We go across to the cupboard where most of my stuff is, and Ryan starts looking. He picks out two polo shirts, passes one to me and slips the other one on himself. It suits him.

"Where do you keep your boxers and stuff, then?"

I open the drawer, and Ryan picks up and considers various pairs of the tight boxers I always wear, before choosing some. He's trying to put them on under his towel, like he's getting changed on the beach or something.

I put my hand on his arm. "Ryan, I don't think we need to worry about…" I untuck my towel and let it fall; my nob is so hard, it's sticking almost straight up in the air. I see Ryan instinctively throw a look over toward Dan, who's back on the bed, concentrating on the laptop screen. "It's okay. He really doesn't mind." I reach out and take hold of Ryan's towel. My eyes flick upward to his face. I want to check he's all right with this first. He gives me a smile and a small nod, and I undo his towel and let it fall.

The excitement of standing there with my dick out, with Dan just across the room, hits me once again. I can't help it. It's such a turn-on, even if he isn't watching.

Suddenly, Dan's voice cuts in, "Get some fucking clothes on, can't you? How can I concentrate on my porno with your dicks bouncing around everywhere?"

I love it when he starts giving out abuse. And so much for him not watching!

"Well, you don't have to look."

"It's hard to ignore it when you're virtually fucking right in front of me, in my room."

"We're not virtually fucking. And it's my room too, remember."

"Look. Get some fucking pants on, get over to his room, and stick that fucking thing where the sun don't shine. Then maybe I can concentrate on this video. You're not the only ones with a boner that needs dealing with, you know."

I grin at him. "Well, if you want to get started now, that's fine with me."

"And me," interjects Ryan.

"Well, you can both fuck right off. I've done enough queer stuff in the last twenty-four hours. I'm not starting on this till you're out of that fucking door."

I'm a bit disappointed, but only a bit. "Okay, okay, we get the idea. We're going."

Ryan puts on the boxers and I rub my hand over the material, feeling him up, as he reaches into the drawer to choose some for me. He holds them open, and I step into them. He pulls them up over my cock and has a quick feel while he does it. This is really hot, and I move in to give him a kiss.

"Fucking stop that." It's Dan.

"Sorry. I forgot. We're going, okay?"

"Today would be good."

"We're almost out the door. Really."

But of course we're not. We need to finish getting dressed first, and that takes a minute or two. Ryan's careful about choosing socks for both of us, and changes his mind a couple of times before he's happy. His Converse are in the pile of wet stuff on the floor, of course, so he chooses a pair of my Adidas for himself.

I look over to the bed. "Dan? Can I wear your DCs again?"

"What?" He looks up. "No. Not if you're going to spunk on them, like yesterday."

"Look. I won't. I promise you."

Ryan's laughing. "You didn't? Fucking hell. But you only met each other yesterday. You jizzed on his trainers when you'd only known him, like, a few hours?"

"Ryan, mate, you have no idea." Dan's going to give him all the details, I can tell. "This guy"—he's pointing at me—"this guy is the biggest pervert I've ever met. He came and stalked me in the SU, made me feel sorry for him, then took my trainers off me and spunked a whole fucking load on them. Then the little cunt tried to give me them back, when they were still fucking wet with his wank juice. I tell you, Ryan, he's a fucking nightmare. You should keep away from him."

I know he's winding me up, and I know Ryan won't care, but I can't stop myself. "Dan, that's so unfair. Ryan, it wasn't like that at all. I mean, I didn't, well, I did sort of…Look, what I mean is…oh fuck it! Shall we just go, before he says anything else?"

Ryan gives me a grin and agrees. I put Dan's trainers on and go over to the bag where I keep my Fleshlight and the other stuff I needed to keep out of sight at home. I look through until I find condoms and lube. The condoms have been in there ages. I hope they haven't gone out of date.

It occurs to me that we might not actually need them. I mean, we're both virgins, I suppose, although I don't know exactly what happened with the guy who attacked Ryan, how far it went, whether—I look across at Ryan, but decide that's definitely not a conversation to have in front of Dan. Instead, I slip some condoms and lube into my jeans pocket. "Right. All set?"

"Yeah, think so."

"Okay, let's go then." We head together to the door and then turn back to Dan. It's a bit of an awkward moment, and I'm not sure what to say.

Dan rescues the situation for us. "Have fun, then. And don't make too much noise. These walls are pretty thin. You don't want to upset Ryan's new neighbors before he's even met them."

We both smile, and I look at Dan and the laptop. "You too. The Fleshlight's in the bag, by the way, if you want it."

Dan considers for a moment. "Hmm, that might be a pretty cool idea."

Ryan opens the door, and I follow him out into the corridor. At the top of the stairs, we both stop and look at each other. Neither of us speaks, but we don't need to. It feels like such a big thing that's about to happen, and we're both so excited that we can hardly keep it in. Ryan looks around quickly to check that the coast is clear, and then pulls my head toward his and kisses me. Then we set off down the stairs and across the grass to Ryan's accommodation block.

When we arrive, there's a note wedged in between the door and the frame. Ryan takes it and unfolds the paper. I suppose it must be from James.

Ryan looks up, mystified. "It's from Security."

"What do you mean, Security?"

"University Security. You know. I suppose it must be the guys who drive round campus in those white vans. There's a phone number. They want me to ring someone called Darren."

"What about?"

"It doesn't say."

Ryan starts to get his phone out and then seems to realize that we're still standing in the corridor, and so finds his key first and lets us in. There's no sign that James has been back, and he's certainly not here now.

Ryan goes to the bed and sits down, starting to tap the number into his phone. I sit next to him, and put a hand on his leg. I can hear the ring tone as I slip my other hand round behind him and up his back, under the polo shirt. I hope this isn't going to take long.

I hear the call connect, but I can't make out much of what's being said at the other end of the line. The call seems to be about James, I think, but it's a bit cryptic. As he talks, Ryan puts his free hand between my legs and moves it up toward my crotch. It feels nice.

Ryan ends the call and gives my leg a squeeze. "It's James," he says. "He's in the medical center. Seems he fell in the lake last night. I think he must have been pissed."

"What? *The* James? The one who lives here—geek of the year?"

"I know. It doesn't sound like him, does it? Still, it must be. He asked someone to get a message to me. He wants me to go and see him."

"Why didn't he ring you?"

"Not sure. I suppose his phone must have fallen in with him."

"I suppose." I'm really pissed off. Why did this have to happen now? "Ryan, can't you go a bit later, you know? I wanted us to have some time on our own. Now, I mean." I move my hand right up Ryan's leg and onto the bulge in his jeans. He lets me do it, but I can tell his mind is elsewhere.

"Tom, I'm sorry. I really want to stay here with you, but I think I ought to go. There's something weird going on with James. Don't know what, exactly, but I've got a bad feeling about it. Look, it won't take long, okay?"

"Yes, I suppose so." I want to argue with him, but I know he's right. If it was me lying in the medical center, with no friends, I'd want someone to come over straightaway. "I'll come with you, all right?"

Ryan looks at me. "Are you sure? You don't have to, you know."

"I want to. It means I'll be with you, which is where I want to be, and if there's two of us, it might be easier to cheer that miserable bastard up a bit."

"Thanks." He gives me a kiss. "And then we can fuck, yeah?"

"Thought we were going to make *lurrrve*?"

"Okay. So you can make *lurrrve* my brains out, for the rest of the day if you want."

We get up, and Ryan goes to look for some clothes for James. Good job Ryan can think about more than one thing at a time; it wouldn't have occurred to me. He stands looking into the cupboard.

"Tom, all his stuff is shit. He doesn't have one decent thing to wear."

I take a look, and he's right. I watch as Ryan picks up a few random things and finds a bag to put them in. Then we head for the door.

The medical center is about a ten-minute walk across campus, and we pass the time mostly talking about James, and comparing him to Dan, not very favorably. At least the rain's stopped, anyway.

We can see James as soon as we go through the main door. He's sitting on a bed in a side room, with the door open. He's wearing pajamas and a dressing gown, and he's staring at the floor. A woman comes over, and Ryan speaks to her briefly, and then we go into James's room. He looks up briefly and then back down. "I didn't know if you'd come. Didn't know if you'd want to."

Ryan steps forward. "Of course we did. Look, we've brought you some clothes, so you can get out of here."

James doesn't look up or speak. Ryan and I catch each other's eye as the silence lengthens and becomes more awkward. Eventually, Ryan speaks. "Er, James. Have we, you know, done something wrong?" Another silence. "Shall we just go?"

"No." He's still looking down, but at least he's said something. "I mean, no, please don't go. I didn't mean to be rude. I was going to ask you something. I've been planning it all morning, but now you're here it feels so stupid. I think it's better if I don't."

"No, mate, go ahead. I'm sure it's not stupid. It'll be fine."
"I can't."

This is getting us nowhere, so I try a different approach. "Look, James. If it's something difficult, let's leave it for a bit, and maybe talk about it later, yeah? Why don't you tell us what happened last night? Did you really fall in the lake?"

Ryan joins in. "Yeah, what happened to you? I just went for a piss and you'd fucked off. I've been worrying about you. Me and Tom went out looking for you this morning. In the rain!"

"Did you? Really?"

"Yeah, we did. Got fucking soaked actually, but it doesn't matter. Come on. Tell what's been going on."

James takes a few deep breaths before he speaks. "Okay. Right. Well, I wasn't coping very well with anything yesterday. I was thinking bad things, and I just needed to get away on my own for a bit."

Ryan looks worried. "Christ, mate, what do you mean, 'thinking bad things'?" He goes to sit on the bed next to James, and I move to the only chair.

"It doesn't matter. I was just…I wanted some time on my own, that's all."

Ryan looks at me. I think he's deciding whether to ask the same question again. He decides against it. "So what happened after you went?"

"I bought a bottle of vodka and went down to the lake."

I'm just about to laugh and make a joke of some sort when I catch the bleak look on James's face, and a shiver goes through me. "Shit, James. What are you saying, for God's sake?"

Once again, there's no answer, and Ryan takes up the questions. "James, did you…did you drink a whole bottle of voddy?"

James looks up briefly. "I drank quite a lot of it, but then I was really sick."

"Fuck. And did you—shit, mate, please tell me you didn't fall in on purpose."

"No. Well, I thought about it, sort of thought about it, anyway, but I didn't."

Ryan looks at me. Neither of us knows what to say, but James goes on. "In the end, I decided to come back and talk to you, Ryan, but I was a bit drunk, and I lost my footing on the edge of the lake."

"A bit drunk? You must have been fucking wasted. Are you used to drinking that much?"

"No. I don't normally drink much. Well, not at all, really."

"But why, mate? I don't understand."

I move forward on my chair. "Is this to do with what you were saying when we got here? About wanting to ask us something? I think it's time you told us the whole story, yeah?"

James is wringing his hands in his lap. "I don't think I can."

"I think you need to talk to someone."

Ryan backs me up. "Yeah, you do. And Tom's a good listener. I know that. I told him some heavy shit yesterday, and I feel loads better now."

James's hands move to his knees, and he breathes deeply again. "Okay. But if I'm going to get through this, I need you...I mean, please, if you don't mind, would you just let me say it all, and not interrupt? It will make it a bit easier."

"Sure. If that helps," says Ryan.

"Well, I don't know where to start, really. Yesterday, I suppose. The reason I was feeling so rubbish yesterday was, well, I thought uni was going to be different, but it isn't. It's just the same thing again."

I'm just about to cut in and ask what he means. I'm not following this at all, but Ryan puts his hand on my leg to shut me up.

"I'm making a mess of this, aren't I? Look, what I mean is, I had a bad time at school. Bullying and all that sort of thing. I didn't really have any proper friends, just a few of the other saddos who I hung about with sometimes."

I interrupt without thinking. "I'm sure you weren't a saddo."

Ryan slaps me on the knee. "Shut up, will you? You're supposed to be listening and not interrupting, remember?"

"Sorry."

"It's okay. And I was a saddo. But look, that's not the point. The point is that I thought uni was going to be different. A fresh start, you know. Lots of new friends. No more problems. But then, when I got here...Well, I found out who I was sharing a room with, and it was just like being back at school."

Oh shit. That's Dan he's talking about. I'm desperate to say something, to try to defend Dan, but I've promised I won't. Instead I take hold of Ryan's hand, which is still resting on my leg, and wait for James to continue.

"I mean, he came in like he owned the place, wearing that T-shirt and swearing all the time. He was just like some of them at school. He even said some of the same things they used to say. And I know I shouldn't have, but I got angry, and that made him get angry. He called me a, well, you know, the c-word. Then he went. So much for everything being different, eh? Nothing was going to be different. I realized it suddenly; just like that. And there wasn't anything I could do about it. Anyway, when he came back, I was already in bed, but I wasn't asleep. I haven't slept much since I got here, actually. But I pretended I was. I couldn't talk to him. I just couldn't. I was too scared. Then after a few minutes, I heard him...I could hear him..." his voice trails off. I look up at him, and I can see the red blush rising up his neck. He's finding this really difficult.

I know I said I wouldn't interrupt, but fuck it. "Look, I know what you're trying to say, so if it's too embarrassing, you don't have to talk about this."

"I do." He sounds quite sure. "He was having...he was masturbating. And I think he was making as much noise as he could, just to embarrass me."

Again, I can't stop myself from jumping in. "Look, James, I know how it must seem. I know you think Dan is a...well, that c-word you mentioned, I expect. But he's not. You ought to give him another chance. I'll talk to him if you like, get him to ease off a bit. He can be a bit hardcore, I admit. I can understand why you hate him, but if I can just—"

"Hate him? I don't hate him."

"Well, maybe that's the wrong word."

"I don't hate him. I want to be like him! Don't you see? I want to be like all three of you. You're all so cool, and you're going to have loads of friends and have a great time here. And you don't even have to try. It just comes naturally to you, and I don't know how to do any of it." James puts his head in his hands and sits perfectly still on the bed. I look at Ryan. He seems to be about as surprised as I am.

I can't think of anything to say. Ryan opens his mouth, but then closes it again. I decide to wait. Eventually, James lifts his head and seems ready to say some more. "I do know I'm different. I watch people all the time, and I know I'm geeky and sad and everything else they used to call me at school. And I've had enough of it. I want to be like everyone else and fit in, but I'm too scared."

"What are you scared of?"

"Everything. Scared of being a loner like this forever. Scared of having to change if I want things to get better. Scared of the cool people. And I'm scared by the way cool people talk and act. You know, people like you. Swearing and talking about sex, all that kind of thing. Anything, you know, even a bit rude—I can't handle it, and I can feel myself getting embarrassed and going red."

"I could see, before, that you were quite embarrassed talking about Dan, you know, him wanking in your room. Is that the kind of thing you mean?"

"I'm like that all the time. Everything about sex makes me get like that. Even saying the words. Why can't I even talk about it? I feel so stupid. I get embarrassed if people are having sex on the telly, or just kissing, even if I'm watching it on my own."

Ryan puts a hand on James's leg. "Mate, don't be so hard on yourself. I'm sure you can get through this. I don't suppose it will be easy, but you just need to, you know, keep working at it."

"That's what I want to do. That's what I've decided. Will you help me, though? I can't do it on my own."

"Help you? What do you mean? I don't see what we can do?"

"I need someone to let me hang around with them, put up with me being there, you know? So I can learn how to fit in better. And I need people to make me face up to things, make me say things when I'm embarrassed to say them. Make me do the things I'm scared of doing, stop me just hiding and running away from stuff."

Ryan looks at me, then back at James. "Of course we'll help. If that's what you want."

"Are you sure you don't mind?"

I give him a smile. "No, we don't mind. If it's going to make you happier, make life seem better for you—"

Ryan cuts in, "Can we start straightaway? Because there's something I've been wanting to say ever since I first saw you."

James looks wary. "Oh God. What is it?"

"It's just about your clothes."

"Oh, yes." James looks down at his hands. "They're not very fashionable, are they?"

"Mate, they're utter shit and you need to bin them."

I can't believe he's just said that. "Ryan, that's really rude. You can't expect—"

But James interrupts. "It's all right. I know I haven't got any decent clothes. I let my mum buy most of what I've got. I did try, sometimes, though. Like last week, before I came away. I went into town to get some new things, but everyone in the shops looked so cool and fashionable, I didn't dare go in. I came back without buying anything. So I know my clothes are a bit rubbish, and you can be as rude as you want."

"Okay, I will." Ryan laughs. "But, hey, mate. No one our age says 'rubbish' like that. We need to get your language sorted out if you want to mix with uber-cool metrosexuals like us."

I snort with laughter, and Ryan grins back at me. Even James manages a smile, the first one I've seen. "So what should I say, then?"

"Shit. Your clothes are shit. In fact, repeat after me, 'All my clothes are shit, and I need to throw the whole fucking lot in the bin.'"

There's a slight pause, while Ryan and I look at James, and his eyes go back and forth between the two of us. Then he takes a deep breath. "Okay. All my clothes are shit." Another breath. "And I need to throw the whole...the whole fucking lot in the bin."

James manages another smile, although he looks like he's on the edge of a panic attack, and the redness is back in his neck and face, big time.

Ryan gives him a round of applause. "There. That wasn't so bad, was it? Right, I think we should get out of this place. I've got a bag of shit clothes here for you to put on. And, Tom, I think you should ring Dan. I hope he hasn't gone to rugby yet. This is a job he needs to help with."

Ten minutes later, we've finished sorting things out with the woman at the medical center, James has put on the shit clothes, and we're all on the way back to my room. I'm explaining things to Dan over the phone. He was just about to go to rugby training, but decides to stay and help with the James project instead. "This sounds like a right fucking laugh."

When we get back to the room, we hang up the phones, and I finish telling Dan about the plan. "So we're going to try and encourage James, yeah, and help him with the stuff he's struggling with. I thought maybe we could start with a trip into town, to look for some clothes. And then gradually start tackling, you know, more difficult things. What do you think?" I turn to James for a reaction, but Dan cuts in before he has time to say anything.

"Fuck that! It's a crap idea. Look, James, mate, you won't get anywhere if you pussy around with this. You've got to just go for it, mate. I mean, like head on."

"Dan, don't start getting pushy. James doesn't need you being all hardcore with him; he just needs some time and some encouragement."

James's voice breaks in. "No, let him say what he wants to. He may be right."

I'm not having this, though. "But I thought we had a plan?"

Dan turns to me. "Yeah, but it's your plan, not ours, and it might just be a shit plan. So James is listening to me now, and you can shut the fuck up, okay?"

I know when I'm beaten. "Okay."

Dan's in full flow now. "Right, mate, the way I see it is, we either fuck about for months 'encouraging' and 'taking our time' like this fucking pussy wants to, or we get all the pain over in one go. It might hurt more, but it'll be over a lot quicker. Like, you've decided your clothes are shit, and, mate, I have to agree with you there. Well, you can either take years changing things one at a time, or you can just go right now and burn the fucking lot, borrow stuff off us, just fucking do it. That's how to deal with it. Same with the things you're embarrassed about. Let's do them all now. We'll make you, if you need us to. Once you've done stuff a few times, you'll be fine. What do you say?"

There's a short pause. I look over at Ryan who shrugs, and then back at James. "James, don't let him boss you round. This sounds like a nightmare."

Another silence, while James thinks. Then, "You're right, Tom. It does sound like a nightmare. It sounds like a complete and total nightmare actually. So let's do it!"

Me and Ryan together, "What?"

"I want to do it the way Dan says. Maximum pain, maximum gain, that's what they say, isn't it? I've been like this for so long, it's going to take a big shock to jolt me out of it."

Dan rubs his hands together. "Right then. What's going to be the best thing to do? I need to think about this one."

I turn back to James. He's looking a bit pale. "James, he's going to suggest something, I don't know, really heavy. Don't let him push you into this."

Instant reply from James, "Shut the fuck up!" I can't believe he's said that, and my mouth drops open.

James's expression changes. His eyebrows rise in alarm. "Sorry. I didn't mean to say that. Sorry. It just came out. I've always wanted to say that to someone, but I've never dared do it. Sorry, though, that was really rude."

I can't help smiling. He's really funny when he's like this. "It's okay. Stop apologizing."

"Okay, okay, I've stopped. Sorry." He pauses for a few deep breaths. "Have I upset you, though?"

"No, James. You haven't upset me. Of course you haven't."

"Are you sure?"

"I'm completely fucking sure."

"Okay, good. Sorry, though. Anyway, can we start on this straightaway? And you all have to help me. And don't let me back out of anything, even if I try to. So what happens now?"

Dan looks round all of us before speaking. "Right, lads. Circle jerk. Let's get naked."

I break out in an immediate grin, and looking across at Ryan, I see that he's grinning too. Dan's voice breaks in again, "Thought you boys would like that idea, you dirty fuckers." I love how this was Dan's idea, but it's me and Ryan who are the dirty fuckers. "Well, come on, then."

I grab at my polo shirt and pull it over my head, but then I notice James. He's just standing there, looking really awkward. "James? Are you going to be okay with this? I know what you said, but you don't have to do this, you know."

James turns to me. He's still looking shit-scared, but there's some determination on his face, too. "I told you. I want to do this. And you have to make sure I do, okay? It sounds scary, but I'm going to do it."

I'm amazed by the look in his eyes. "You really are, aren't you? Fucking hell."

"There is one thing though." James looks round all of us in turn. "What *is* a circle jerk exactly?"

I really want to laugh, but I manage to stop myself. That really wouldn't help James. I look at Dan, but he's leaving this one to me. "You better tell him all about it, Tom. I'm getting some porn running on this thing." And he heads across to where his laptop is still open on the bed. "Some of us might need it, even if you don't."

I look at Ryan, who just grins. Looks like nobody's going to help me out here, so I plunge in. "Well, James, okay. So we all stand in a circle, yeah, all facing into the middle. And then we all have a wank. And then we all, you know, spunk up. That's kind of it, really."

"No, not really! You missed the most important bit." Dan's finished logging in to the laptop, and he's heading back across to us, pulling his rugby shirt over his head. "Tom's just a little, cocksucking queer; he doesn't know anything about proper, manly, straight stuff like circle jerks. Thing is, you don't wank yourself off, mate, you wank the guy next to you, okay?" Just when I think I can't be surprised by anything else Dan says or does, he comes out with that.

Ryan's the first to respond. "Fucking hell, this is going to be so hot. I want to wank Tom. Which side of him do I have to go?"

Dan thinks carefully about this for a while. "No, Ryan, mate, I don't think that's a good plan. You two'll start getting overexcited, and me and James don't want to end up watching you slobbering all over each other. We're going to keep you apart. By the way, Ryan, has he fucked you yet?"

Oh shit, not that again. "Fuck's sake, Dan, I told you not to keep saying stuff like that."

"Why not?"

"Because it's embarrassing—for James, I mean."

"For you, you mean. Anyway, James wants maximum embarrassment so he can get over it quicker, don't you, mate?" James manages a nod, although the redness is back in his face and neck. Dan continues, "So, Ryan, yes or no?"

Ryan gives him a huge grin. "No. Not yet. But soon, eh?" And he reaches out and rubs his hand over the front of my jeans, feeling up my nearly hard cock through the denim.

"Okay, okay, that's enough of that. Get some clothes off, then. Got to be naked to do this properly." Dan sticks both hands down the front of his rugby shorts, and starts massaging his cock into life. It's fucking hot watching him, and when he pulls the shorts down and reveals a nearly hard cock, I realize that I've still got most of my clothes on. I reach for my belt as a naked Dan goes over to James. "So, mate. Still up for this?"

"Yes."

"Ever had a wank in front of anyone before?"

"No! God, no. I've never even talked about it."

"But you do it though? I mean, you do have wanks?"

James takes another deep breath. "Yes. Yes, I do."

"And you enjoy it?"

"Well, yes. I suppose I do, yes."

"Only 'suppose'?"

"No. I'm sure. I do enjoy doing it. Quite a lot actually."

"How often?"

"What?"

"How often do you have a wank?"

"Oh. God. Well, every day, I suppose. At least one every day. Is that normal?"

"Sounds fucking normal to me."

"Thank God for that. Sometimes I think I'm probably doing it too much, and maybe there's something wrong with me."

"Can't do it too much, mate. No such thing as too much wanking." And then after a pause, "In my humble opinion." He grins round at us. "So. All ready then?"

Ryan moves forward. "Before we start, I think James should say what's happening, you know, out loud. Because he managed to get through that whole conversation without saying any of the embarrassing words, and we're supposed to be helping him with that."

Dan nods. "Yeah, that's right. Come on, then, James, what's about to happen?"

"Well, oh God. Right. We're going to stand in a circle and…and wank each other."

"Good. And what's going to happen to you after you've got wanked off for a bit?"

"I'm, er, I'm going to cum."

"Brilliant. You're doing a fucking good job here. And when you cum, what's going to come out of your dick?"

"Oh Jesus. You're not going to make this easy, are you? Okay, right. Well, there's going to be…I, er, what should I call it?"

"Call it spunk, mate."

"Okay. So when I cum, there's going to be spunk coming out of my dick. Shit!" He looks terrified, but he's done it.

"Cool. See? It's not as bad as you thought."

"It is. It's a nightmare, like I said, but I haven't run away yet, and it will get easier, won't it?"

"Yep, it will. So you think you're going to manage to get a hard-on, mate?"

"Well, I've, er, well I've got a bit of one already."

"Good lad."

I'm just taking off my boxers and watching as Ryan does the same with his, when Dan's voice cuts in again. "Fucking hell!"

I swing round to find him staring at James's crotch. James has got as far as undoing his trousers, and the shape of his nob is unmistakable in his boxers. It's enormous, pulling the waistband right up, and twitching in time with his pulse. What did he just say? "A bit of a hard-on"? For fuck's sake.

Dan seems very impressed too. "Have you seen this, lads? It's a fucking weapon. You could beat someone up with that."

James seems surprised. "I thought it was, you know, about average. I haven't really seen many. Well, none, actually."

"Believe me, mate. That's a fucking monster. Once the girls hear about that, you're going to get so much sex. Fucking hell. Right, we ready yet?" Dan goes over to the laptop and turns the volume up to maximum. I can't see the screen from where I am, but the sounds of women getting fucked start coming across loud and clear. When he comes back to us, he's ready to take charge, and I for one, am quite happy to let him. "So I'm going here and James opposite. Okay, mate? Tom, over here." He takes me by the shoulders and moves me into position and then does the same with Ryan.

In the circle, I'm standing with Ryan opposite me. Both our cocks are completely hard, and Ryan's rubbing his gently as he looks from one of us to another. Dan's on my right, and James is on my left. James's weapon is jerking about of its own accord, his face and neck are very red, and he's shifting nervously from foot to foot. I can tell he wants to move his hands in front of his cock and cover it up, but he's doing a good job of stopping himself. Dan seems happy with the arrangement. "Right, lads, I think we just need to snuggle up a bit."

"Hang on." I've had a sudden thought. "I'll get some lube." I run across to my bag, find a fresh container, and rip the cellophane off. I'm back in the circle in a few seconds. I hold out the lube to Dan, as I feel like he's in charge of this. He doesn't take it, though. "You first, Tom, mate. Go on."

I pump the nozzle a few times until I've got a big, sticky gloop of lube in my right hand, and then reach out and take hold of Dan's nob. It feels great, touching it again, and I love how it gets harder as I start to massage the lube in, and to slowly wank my hand up and down the shaft.

Dan reaches across and takes the lube, squeezing out a ridiculous amount into his palm. He's got enough to lube up the whole of Ryan, but I suppose it doesn't matter. As Dan's hand closes round Ryan's cock, Ryan goes into porn star mode. "Oh, that feels sooo good. Fucking give it to me!" He's still got the huge grin on his face; he's loving this.

Now it's Ryan's turn to take the lube. He squeezes some out and then looks at James. "You ready for this? Just fucking enjoy yourself, yeah?"

James looks back steadily at him. "Yes, just do it. I mean, just fucking do it." When Ryan's hand takes hold of his cock, James's whole body stiffens for a moment, and then he closes his eyes and breathes deeply, willing himself to relax. One of his legs is shaking badly. His eyes open, and he watches as Ryan rubs his hand round and round his bell-end, and then he reaches for the lube. He squirts some into his palm, looks at it, and holds his hand out toward me. "Is that enough?"

"Looks fine to me."

James reaches out and takes hold of my cock, just holding for a few seconds, while he calms his nerves, and while a woman on the laptop screams at the top of her voice that she's cumming. Then James's hand starts to move slowly up and down my cock. Dan seems to take that as a signal for us all to start, and he begins wanking Ryan properly. Ryan and I join in. This is fucking amazing. I just watch the four hands and the four cocks for a few seconds, enjoying every second. The feel of Dan's hard, shiny nob in my hand again. The sight of Ryan's naked body opposite me, starting to react to what Dan's doing to him.

Suddenly, a noise from James, "Oh God!"

Shit, I think he's going to cum. We've only been going a few seconds. Ryan realizes what's happening and starts wanking him faster. Almost immediately, there's a big grunt from James, and a huge rope of spunk shoots across the circle and lands on Dan's chest, followed by a second one, equally big, which goes right down my leg and onto my foot. He seems to cum for ages. We've all got some of it on us. Ryan's hand is covered in it.

Dan grins at him. "Think you needed that, mate."

James smiles back. "Wow. I don't know what to say."

"Was it okay?"

"Yeah, I suppose it was. Not as bad as I thought. And rubbing that stuff on first was good. It felt amazing actually."

"No, James, it felt *fucking* amazing."

"Oh, yes, I forgot. Sorry. It felt *fucking* amazing. Now shut the fuck up, all of you, while I do this…" And he grabs my dick again and starts wanking it so hard I have to bite my lip to stop myself from shouting out. Good job he put plenty of lube on. I'm trying to think about getting a rhythm going on Dan's nob again, but what James is doing is so intense that I can't really concentrate on anything else. It's only a minute or so until I feel my balls starting to pull up inside my sack and my orgasm starts.

"Going to cum," I manage to blurt out, not that it makes any difference. James isn't going to slow down or be put off now; if anything, he even speeds up a bit more. I see Ryan move forward a bit. He obviously wants this load on him, and he fucking gets it. Right up his chest, nearly to his shoulder, then on his cock and Dan's hand, and then some on his leg. In the end, I feel the cum starting to subside, and I put my hand on James's wrist to slow him down. James stops wanking me and lets go of my nob, holding his hand in front of him to look at the spunky mess I've left on it. Suddenly, Ryan reaches out, takes James's hand and lifts it up to his face. He catches my eye for a second, and then sucks the whole lot straight off James's hand. He looks round again, registering the expressions on everyone's faces. "What?"

Dan shakes his head. "Fucking queers. Nightmare. Anyway, what the fuck's happened to my wank? Some of us haven't finished yet." With that, he gets to work on Ryan again, and I turn my attention back to Dan.

There's still plenty of lube on his cock, which means I can rub my hand right up and over the head, as well as up and down the shaft. He seems to be enjoying it; he's tensing up and breathing quite hard, his abs pulling in and out as he breathes. After a couple of minutes, he speaks, "You getting anywhere near, Ryan, mate? Could we try and cum at the same time?"

Ryan's breathing hard too. He lifts his arms and puts one across James's shoulders and the other across Dan's. "Yeah, close. Just a bit faster, and I'll be—oh fuck!" His whole body clenches and tightens, and he goes up on his toes as the orgasm takes hold of him. But I mustn't watch Ryan. I need to concentrate on Dan, and try to get him to cum too. I speed up my hand until it's almost a blur. I notice a big squirt of Ryan's spunk landing on my other hand and arm, but I'm too busy to take much notice. Then I feel Dan's arm move onto my shoulder, and his body starts to tense and jerk next to me— here it comes. And James gets the whole fucking lot. He just stands there and lets it land on him, squirt after squirt, without even flinching.

When I feel Dan's body starting to relax, and the pressure from his arm on my shoulder eases, I slow down my hand, and gradually bring it to a stop. We're all breathing very hard and looking round at each other's bodies, at the patterns of the splashes and spots of cum that are all over us.

I feel something rubbing against my leg, and when I look down, Dan's wiping his bell-end against my thigh. "Fuck's sake, Dan."

"What's the matter, queer boy? Don't you like spunk any more?"

Ryan reaches out and transfers the little trail of Dan's cum onto his finger. "Well, I do. I'll have it." He transfers the finger to his mouth and licks it extravagantly. "Mmm, tasty." He grins at me across the circle.

Everyone's breathing is starting to return to normal, and everyone is covered in rapidly cooling goo. It's probably time to go and get cleaned up. I suggest hitting the showers, and wonder if Ryan will want to share the shower again. But Dan isn't having any of that. "Hold on. I don't think so." He goes over to the bed and picks up a big towel. "Wipe up the worst of it with this." He throws the towel to me. "We're only halfway through. A few minutes to watch some porn and recover, and it'll be time for round two!"

CHAPTER NINE

It's already an hour since we had the circle jerk, and there's no sign of "round two" yet.

Dan's on a mission, though. He's watched some porn with James, while Ryan and I cuddled on the bed for a bit, then he rolled a massive joint, which we took turns on, trying to blow the smoke out the window. James, of course, hadn't smoked before—even ciggies—and he didn't have much of the joint, but he's gone a bit quiet. I wonder what he's thinking.

Then Dan just fucked off. He said he needed to get something and wouldn't say what it was. Ryan and I both tried to find out what he was planning, but he just told us we'd find out soon enough.

So now, James is sitting on Dan's bed with the laptop, and I'm lying next to Ryan, playing with his nob a bit, and wondering what it'll be like when I finally get to fuck him. Maybe it'll happen tomorrow, if nothing else goes wrong.

James's voice cuts in, "I was wondering, well, there's something I want to do."

"Yeah?"

"Well, you know all my shit clothes…I, er, I want to get rid of them. Now, I mean, before I change my mind. But that's going to mean borrowing things off you three for a bit, you know, until I get some new ones. Will that be okay?"

Ryan looks up at him. "Of course, mate, no problem. Borrow what you want."

James looks relieved. "Thanks. I didn't know if you'd mind or not. Can we go and do it now?"

"Now?"

"If that's okay. There's a big recycling place round the back of the medical center. I saw it when we came out this morning. I'm going to put everything in the clothes recycling, in case anyone else wants it."

Ryan breaks into a big grin. "Mate, I don't think they will. I mean, I know some people are desperate, but well…"

"Fuck off!"

I look up at James. It still seems a bit weird when he swears like that, and he's got an expression like a little kid who's just sworn at his mum, and he's waiting to see if he gets a slap or not. James looks at Ryan and then at me. We're both grinning. Once he's sure we're still okay with him, he puts the laptop down on the bed next to him and gets up. He starts putting on clothes—the same ones Ryan took to the medical center for him, earlier on. Ryan and I get up too and start to dress. There's dried spunk all over my leg and arm, and my skin feels tight when I move, but I suppose it doesn't matter. Before we go, I text Dan to let him know what's happening.

A couple of minutes later, we're back in James's room, and he's ramming all his stuff into some carrier bags he's found in his wardrobe. He's gone a bit manic.

I go over to him. "James, you don't have to get rid of everything. When Ryan said about throwing all your clothes in the bin, he didn't mean literally everything. You might want to keep some things."

James doesn't even look up from stuffing a handful of socks into the bag. "No, I don't. I want to get rid of all of it. It's all shit, and I want to start again. So. Ready?"

I look into the empty wardrobe. "Yeah, I suppose so. As long as you're sure."

"I'm sure."

The whole thing has only taken about two minutes, and we're on our way again. James is going so fast, I'm almost having to jog to keep up with him. It doesn't take long to get to the recycling bins.

James turns to face us. "Right. This is it, then. Good-bye old, shit clothes, and old, shit life." I can't help thinking how funny and melodramatic this sounds. I try unsuccessfully to look serious, but James doesn't seem to notice. He starts trying to force the bulging carrier bags into the narrow slot on the bin, without much success, and Ryan goes across and helps him. They're gone in a few moments, and the metal lid of the bin clangs shut. I can see James's shoulders rise and fall as he takes a deep breath.

Ryan pats him on the back. "Well done, mate. That's all sorted, then."

"Not quite."

"What do you mean?"

"That's not quite all of it." James reaches up, grabs the collar of his shirt, rips it off over his head and rams it into the metal slot. Ryan laughs and then looks around to see if anyone's in sight. Then James reaches down, takes off the shiny brown shoes, and sends them to follow the rest of his stuff.

There's a look in his eye that is worrying me a bit. "Fuck's sake, James. I think you'd better stop there, eh? You're going to get arrested if you take off anything else."

But James isn't going to stop. Before Ryan or I can do anything about it, he's taken off his trousers and they're disappearing into the bin. He takes hold of the waistband of his boxers just as Ryan and I reach him and grab hold of his arms. "James! Stop, you twat. You can't get naked out here. What if somebody sees you?"

James is struggling to get his pants off, and we're holding on to his arms. Thank fuck there's no one around. But he's not giving in. "Dan told me to do everything straightaway and not to be a fucking pussy. So I am."

"But you'll get—I mean, what if—" Then I realize there's no point arguing. It isn't going to do any good. I let go of his arm. "Do what you want. You're a fucking psycho. If anyone asks me, I'm going to say I don't know you."

James finishes the job. His boxers and socks disappear into the recycling bin. Fucking hell, his nob's big. Even now, when it isn't at all hard, it's still massive.

Ryan's voice cuts across my thoughts. "So how are you getting back to the room then, mate?"

There's a pause. James seems to be thinking about this carefully. "We're quite a long way away, aren't we?"

"Yeah, quite a long way."

"And I haven't got any clothes on, have I?"

"No, none at all."

Another longer pause, and then, "Fuck. Double fuck! Why did you let me take all my clothes off? This is the most stupid thing I've ever done in my life."

I look at Ryan. He's almost doubled over laughing, with one hand stuffed in his mouth to try to stop any noise coming out. I shouldn't have looked at him, because now I start laughing too. James turns back to the bin and tries to get his arm into the slot. In a few seconds, he pulls it out again. "It's no good, everything's gone too far down. I can't reach it. What am I going to do?"

Ryan wipes his eyes with the back of his hand. "Look, mate, we'll sort things out. Don't worry. Er…" He takes a quick look around. "We'll go back through the trees and up past the lake. We won't see anyone that way, well, probably not. I'll go and check it's all clear."

With that, Ryan sets off at a crouching run across the car park, looking a bit like a commando, except with no muscles and an emo fringe flopping around. He stops at the corner of the medical center and peers round. Then he beckons, and we set off, as fast as we can. James has got his hands round his tackle. He looks like something out of a seventies comedy show. If I ever tell anyone about this, they won't believe me!

We reach Ryan at the corner, and he looks round and runs off again. It takes a while, but we eventually get back to the accommodation block where my room is. We've just got the last bit to do now, up the stairs and along the corridor. Ryan creeps in through the front door and looks around. He checks in both directions down the ground floor corridor, and then starts up the stairs. He turns to us. "Think it's okay," he whispers, and we move forward to the bottom of the stairs. Suddenly, the door at the top slams open, a loud female laugh sounds out, and two girls start coming down. They're obviously in a hurry. We've got about a second, literally. There's no time to do anything.

The girls reach the bottom of the stairs and look at us. Ryan and I have just managed to shove James back against the wall and to stand in front of him. We're shoulder to shoulder and trying to look natural, but it's a bit obvious that there's a naked guy standing behind us.

Ryan manages a smile. "All right, girls?"

One of them moves her head to the side, trying to get a better look, and Ryan and I lean over to keep the view blocked as much as we can. "Yeah, I think so," she says, "You?"

Ryan waves an arm vaguely. "Yeah, yeah, we're fine."

There's an awkward pause, and the girls look at each other. I'm willing them to go, but they don't seem to want to.

Eventually, the second one breaks the silence. "Has he, er, got no clothes on?"

I don't know why she's asking us, not James. Perhaps she thinks he's weird, or a bit of a retard, or something. I'm not quite sure what to say. "Well, it's funny you should say that, because, well, it might look that way, but, er, actually—"

"Why hasn't he got any clothes on?" The question kind of hangs in the air.

Ryan comes up with a stroke of genius. "It's a kind of initiation thing. Like a dare. You know."

The second girl steps a bit closer. "Really? What does he have to do?" She looks at James and gives him a bit of a smile. "What are they making you do?"

James is completely lost, and, looking over my shoulder, I can see redness spreading up his neck and into his face. Ryan steps in again. "He, er, well, we were doing drinking games, and he lost, so he had to take all his clothes off and run to the medical center and back."

Girl number two is definitely interested. "So is he like, completely naked behind there? I mean completely?" She's having a really good go at getting a look, and Ryan and I are having to keep moving to stop her seeing too much.

Fortunately, at last, her friend steps in. "Katie, stop being such a perv. We need to go."

Katie seems keen to stay, though. "I'm not being a perv. I'm just interested in what the boys are up to, that's all." She gives James a big smile. I think he's pulled.

Her friend persists, though. "Katie, we'll miss the bus."

"Okay, okay." She turns back to us. "I expect I'll see you guys around somewhere soon. I hope I recognize you with clothes on." She's smiling at James again as her friend takes hold of her arm and pulls her away. The front door swings closed, and James lets his breath out noisily.

Ryan turns to him. "I think you're in there, mate. Did you see the way she was looking at you?"

James doesn't reply; he's very red and looking down.

Ryan starts checking the corridors again. "You ready to make a run for it, mate? Just got this last bit to do? James? You okay?"

James is still looking down. "Slight problem, actually."

"What's up?"

"I've got a little bit of an erection." Ryan and I both look down together, to where James has his hands clasped together over his crotch. He's trying his best, but his hands just aren't big enough to cover everything, and there's a big, red bell-end sticking out. I snigger.

"Don't laugh! It's not funny. I couldn't help it. I could see right down her top. And she was…she kept smiling at me, you know?"

Ryan starts up the stairs. "Let's get inside before anyone else comes. And before you poke someone's eye out with that fucking thing." He opens the door at the top of the stairs, looks round, and beckons to us. A few seconds later and we're back in the room, and James is able to let go of his nob, which is still pretty hard, and sticking straight out in front of him.

Ryan looks at it for a bit. "You know? That really is massive. Fucking hell." He shakes his head. "Tell you what, though. It'd look even bigger if you did a bit of pruning."

James looks completely lost. "What?"

"Trim your pubes, mate. It'll make your nob look even bigger. When that Katie gets to see it, she'll fucking faint!"

"Is that what you do with yours?" Ryan nods. "I was wondering why none of you had very much, you know, down there. I noticed before."

Ryan turns to me. "Tom, have you got any clippers?"

"No, but my razor's got a beard trimmer thing on it. He could use that."

James looks really worried. "A razor?"

"James. It's all right. It's an electric one. It's safe. You're not going to cut your nob off or anything."

"I don't know. It sounds a bit risky."

Ryan steps in. "Look, mate, it'll be fine. If you don't fancy doing it yourself, I'm sure Tom'll do it for you, if you ask nicely."

Fucking right. That sounds like a great idea.

But James doesn't seem convinced. "I don't know. I mean, I'm not being rude or anything, but I'm not sure Tom's a very responsible person."

I can't help laughing. "Well, you're right there, I'm not. But I promise to take care of your nob, okay? Your penis will be safe in my hands!" Now Ryan's laughing too.

James takes a moment to make up his mind. "Okay then, let's do it!"

I go and fetch my razor and get the trimmer attached. By the time I've got it sorted out, Ryan's got James sitting on a towel on the edge of the bed. He's got his hands over his bollocks.

"James, you'll have to move your hands."

"All right, but be careful."

I move forward and kneel down between James's legs. His nob is more or less soft now, and I suppose it's about as small as it ever gets. I put out my hand and take hold of it, looking up at James to see how he reacts. He doesn't catch my eye; he's too busy watching what's about to happen to his dick. I'm wondering where to start. I usually do mine when it's hard—it's easier that way—but I suppose it won't be a problem. I flick the switch on the shaver and bring it up to James's right bollock, holding his nob out of the way with my other hand. The shaver glides over his sack as I hold the skin stretched tight, and the hair starts to fall away.

Immediately, the vibration gets to James. He shudders slightly, and his nob starts to harden really fast. I can feel it filling out in my hand. Before I've even done half his ball sack, he's proper hard. "You're liking this, then?"

"Well, it feels a bit strange. But it's quite nice, actually."

"Cool. Just open your legs a bit more and enjoy it, then."

I go back to work, moving gradually up and round his nob. I can feel the blood pumping into it, and it's super hard. I can't resist the temptation to give it a bit of a wank while I'm shaving it. James doesn't say anything, and he doesn't stop me.

I look up at him again. "I'm not taking too much off, okay? Don't want to look all shaved like a porn star, do you?"

James grins and inspects everything carefully. "You're right. It does make it look bigger. Do you really think that girl, that Katie. Do you really think she was, you know…"

Ryan comes over. "Yeah, she was, mate. She was well up for it."

James looks doubtful. "I'm sure she wasn't." But his grin tells another story, and his nob's twitching even harder. I move the shaver round and start the last bit.

I'm just finishing up when I hear the door open, and I hear Dan's voice. "Oh for fuck's sake! Leave the guy alone, Tom, you fucking—" Then he stops and I turn my head. "Oh shit. Sorry, mate. I thought you were sucking him off. It just looked like it. I came in through the door and you had your fucking head between his legs."

"Dan. Do you really think I'd do that? What kind of a person do you think I am?"

Dan raises an eyebrow and starts to open his mouth to answer, but I cut him off. "Okay, no. Don't answer that. It was a stupid question. Anyway, I'm not. So just stay quiet while I finish this."

I sense Dan coming over as I do the last bits of stray hair. "It looks better, mate. Makes your nob look even bigger, you cunt."

Dan waits until everything's finished and then holds up a paper bag. "Here we go then, lads." He reaches in and pulls out a big chocolate cookie, which he holds up like he's an explorer and he's found some ancient treasure. "Biscuit game. Everyone up for it?"

We all look round at each other. James is the first to answer. "Well, I am. And before you say anything, I *do* know what the biscuit game is. I read something about it on the Internet."

Dan laughs. "Were you looking up dirty stuff on the Web? I didn't think you'd have done that kind of thing."

"I didn't do it on purpose. I was doing a search for a band my sister liked, and I spelled 'biscuit' the wrong way. Anyway, it means I know what we have to do. We all have to, er, to have a wank and make it go on the biscuit. That's right, isn't it?"

Dan looks impressed. "Yeah, mate, spot on. You missed one important bit, though. It's like a race, so the one who cums last has to eat the whole fucking lot."

I look at James, but he doesn't look very concerned. "That's fine. As I'm not going to be the last, I don't have to worry, do I?"

Dan grins. "Top man! Anyway, I don't think either of us have got anything to worry about. This dirty little cum-slut"— and he points at me—"he'll probably be last on purpose. Four loads at once, eh, Tom, you fancy that?"

"Fuck off. Anyway I want you to be last, Dan. I can't wait to see you eating all that creamy cum."

"No chance of that, mate. I reckon I'll be first or second. Oh, and you two"—he waves a finger at me and Ryan—"no helping each other out. You're not allowed to touch each other's dicks, okay? You've got enough of an unfair advantage anyway, you fucking queers."

Dan puts the cookie down, and goes over to the bed, where he reaches for the laptop. He beckons James across, and I realize it's obviously porn time, to get them in the mood. I go to the computer, and Ryan comes to sit next to me. I scroll down through my video files and find a really good one. Soon we're watching two really fit guys fucking on a settee in some skanky council flat. The guys are really getting into it, and I'm really into watching them. Looking at the bulge in Ryan's jeans, he's liking it too.

I glance over at Dan, and he's got his hand in his trackies. "Dan! Get your hand out of there. No wanking yet."

"I'm not wanking. I'm just having a bit of a feel."

"Well, don't. Not until we start properly."

"Fuck's sake. It's only a game. Don't get all arsey on me." But he's smiling, and he takes his hand out of his pants.

I look over to James, who's staring at the screen, with his dick jerking about so hard it's almost banging against his stomach. "I think we better start before he cums over that porno."

Dan looks at him as well, and grins. "Okay. Let's do it."

James is already naked, and it doesn't take long for the rest of us to get our clothes off too. I watch as Dan's hot body gets revealed again. Fucking hell, he's so fit. His nob's not as big as James's, but his body's just perfect. The porn's obviously done its job. All four of us are hard and ready to go. Dan fetches a little bedside cabinet and sets it in the middle of the room, and then gets the cookie and puts it down on top. We all move in closer. I've got Dan opposite me, and Ryan and James on either side.

Dan looks round at all of us. "Right then. All set? Three, two, one!"

He makes a grab for his dick, and starts wanking it so hard it must hurt. I take hold of mine, and start working on it, building up speed. I'm just getting really into it when James starts making a lot of noise. Fucking hell. I think he's going to cum already. He moves a bit closer to the table and tries to point the end of his dick at the cookie. He makes a big grunt, and the spunk starts shooting out. Most of it misses the cookie completely; some of it clears the little table completely and goes on Ryan.

I look over at Dan and think about him having to eat all that spunk and ours too. I get a real jolt of excitement thinking about that, for some reason, and I start wanking a bit faster. I don't think it's going to take me long...

I need another thought, something proper horny to get the cum flowing really fast. I look at Ryan, his hand flying up and down his nob, breathing hard, his stomach pulling in and out, and think, he wants me to fuck him. He wants my cock right inside him. I get a picture of Ryan lying on his back, lifting his legs in the air, holding his ankles, and saying, "Do it, Tom. Fucking do it."

That's all I need. Just thinking about how amazing it's going to be to fuck Ryan sends me straight over the edge. I feel the orgasm starting and move closer in. I manage to get my dick pointing down a bit, so the first shot of cum goes right across the cookie. I feel my legs start to wobble, and I have to put my other hand out to steady myself, as the cum keeps flowing and, eventually, the intensity of the feeling starts to subside.

Once I'm done, I step back and take a look at Ryan and Dan, who are still pumping away. I can hear both of them breathing hard now, but I don't think either of them is that close to cumming.

I decide it's time to help Ryan out. "Ryan, do you want to know what I was thinking about just then, when I was cumming? I was imagining fucking you. I was imagining you lying there, wanting my cock inside you. Does that sound good?"

Ryan gasps a reply as his hand keeps pumping up and down. "You know it does, Tom. Keep talking like that. Make me cum."

"I want you to lie on your back and put your legs up on my shoulders so I can look at you while we're fucking. Would you like that?"

"Fuck, yeah. Can we do it soon?"

But suddenly Dan's voice breaks in, "Shut the fuck up, will you? Stop talking about gay shit. You're putting me off."

"Oh, Dan. I'm so sorry. Looks like you're going to have all this cum to eat after all."

"Fuck you."

Grinning, I turn back to Ryan. "Come on, Ryan, just imagine what it's going to be like to cum with my cock inside you."

Ryan looks up at me. "It's going to be fucking amazing. Tom, I'm so close to cumming, but I can't fucking make it happen. Think I've cum too much today."

"You can do it. Just think the dirtiest thing you can think of."

"I am! It isn't working."

He's still going at it full speed. I'm worried he's going to make it sore if this goes on much longer. I decide it's time for desperate measures. I get my finger and start rubbing it around my bell-end, where there's still quite a lot of fresh spunk, and when it's well lubed up, I step closer to Ryan. I hold up the finger where he can see it, and then move it behind him. "Open up, babe. Coming in."

Ryan bends his knees, I find his arsehole with the tip of my finger and then push it in. It slides in quite easily, and I hear Ryan gasp. I start to move my finger around a bit, and immediately feel Ryan's muscles tightening up, and his body jerks and goes rigid. The spunk starts to flow. It doesn't shoot; it comes out in a sort of stream. Most of it misses the cookie, but what the fuck? Ryan's orgasm seems to go on and on, his body clenching and relaxing for what seems like ages.

Suddenly, Dan's voice again, "You can't fucking do that! That's cheating. I said you couldn't help each other."

"You said no touching each other's dicks. And I didn't touch his dick."

"You know what I meant, you cheating little cunt. I didn't say, 'No sticking your finger up his fucking arse,' because I didn't think even you would do anything that disgusting."

"Well, it's tough shit. You lost, so man up. It's biscuit time."

Ryan picks up the cookie and starts to wipe some of the cum splashes off the top of the cabinet with his finger, and then transfer them to the biscuit.

But Dan isn't giving up that easily. "There is no way I'm eating that shit. You cheated and you can all fuck right off."

I turn to James. "What do you think, then? Can we have your impartial opinion on this?"

James looks back and forth between me and Dan. "Well, I think there are significant arguments to be made on both sides." I find myself laughing, without intending to. Ryan's grinning too. James goes on, "But I think, all things considered, we should pin him down on the floor and force the whole thing into his mouth!"

I high five Ryan. "James, you are so right. I've always said, haven't I, what a sound bloke you are."

Dan steps forward. "Don't you even think about fucking—" But before he can get any further, we all pile on top of him. Dan goes down under the weight of the three of us, and we start trying to get his hands pinned to his sides. Dan's fighting quite hard, but I don't think he's giving it one hundred percent. By the time we've got him under control, most of the spunk's been shaken off the cookie, and even though we manage to force some into Dan's mouth, he spits most of it back out again. It the end, we're all lying in a heap, panting and exhausted.

Ryan starts to laugh, and it quickly spreads to all of us. It feels so brilliant, lying in this pile of naked male bodies, enjoying our closeness and recovering from the exertions of the last few minutes. I let my fingers run through Ryan's hair, and feel his chest rise and fall as he breathes.

"Well, what I think is…" It's James who's first to speak. "I think that since Dan was such a bad loser, and because he didn't actually eat any of the, you know, the spunk, I think he should have to do something else. A forfeit. Like when you told those girls I had to run naked to the medical center and back. Something like that."

Dan looks completely amazed. "What the fuck are you on about?"

I'm not sure I can be arsed to explain at the moment. "Oh, James got naked and pulled this girl. That's all."

Dan's eyes open even wider. "That's all? He seriously got naked and pulled a girl? Like, a real girl?"

"Yes, a real girl."

"When? How? I mean, tell me what happened."

But James isn't letting this go on any longer. "Dan, shut up and stop trying to change the subject. I did get naked, and we did see some girls downstairs, and Ryan and Tom thought one of them liked me, but I'm not sure about that. And then I got a bit of an erection, but it was all right because Tom and Ryan were standing in front of me, so the girls couldn't see it." He stops for breath, and seems to remember what he was planning to say. "Anyway, that's not the point. I think you should do a forfeit to make up for being a bad loser. A fucking bad loser actually, and I'm not going to let you change the subject again."

Dan tries a bit of a protest. "That's so unfair! Those two cheated so badly. They should have to do something, not me."

It sounds a bit feeble, and James isn't having any of it. "That's complete rubbish. They didn't cheat, and you deserve a forfeit."

All of us look at Dan. He shrugs and says nothing.

James presses on. "What shall we make him do, then?'

I'm really not sure what to say. I mean, we've done some pretty mad stuff already, and I can't think of anything else to suggest. "James, I don't know. Have you got any ideas?"

"Not really. Well, I can think of things, but nothing very good." He's clearly giving it some serious thought.

Suddenly, Ryan speaks. "I know what I want him to do." I look across to him, but when our eyes meet, he immediately looks down. "But I don't know what you'll think, Tom. You'll probably hate the idea."

"What do you mean?"

"Can I…look, guys, I want to talk to Tom for a minute, okay?" He looks quite serious, and I can't imagine what the fuck he's thinking about. Ryan guides me over to the window and puts his head quite close to mine so he can talk quietly. It's all a bit weird. "So, right…" He looks across to where Dan is standing and then back at me. "Well, it's just, there's something I've always wanted to do, but it's really pervy. I don't know why I'm even telling you. You'll think I'm a freak."

"Ryan, I doubt it. I don't think your fantasies are going to be any worse than mine." I think back to yesterday and me shooting my load in Ryan's Converse.

"Okay, then. Well, I've always wanted to make a porno film. No, I don't mean make one. I mean be in one."

I think I know where this might be going, and I break out in a big smile straightaway. I nod at Ryan for him to carry on.

"I was thinking that, if you wanted to…I mean, only if you really wanted to, yeah…maybe we could get Dan to film us."

"Film us doing what, exactly?" My grin gets even bigger, and I know what Ryan's going to say, but I want to hear him say it anyway.

"Well, film us fucking. Film our first time, you know. You, fucking me for the first time."

I'm so excited, I can hardly control myself. My cock gives a big twitch, and I feel a big glob of pre-cum oozing out. I take hold of my bell-end and point it up toward Ryan, where it glistens in the light. "That's what my cock thinks of your idea."

"Seriously?"

"Ryan, it's the best idea ever. It's fucking mental! Do you think he'll do it?"

Dan's voice cuts in before Ryan can answer, "Do what? What fucking gay shit do you want me to do this time?"

Ryan laughs. "Actually, mate, you don't have to do any gay shit at all. You just have to film me and Tom doing some."

"What?"

"You have to film us having sex. That's all."

There's quite a long time when no one says anything, and Dan looks back and forth between me and Ryan. Then he looks at James, and back to us. "Okay. Doesn't sound too bad, actually. Thought it would be something much worse than that. As long as you don't try and make me join in or anything." He gives a bit of a shudder. "Fucking hell." Then a new thought seems to hit him. "And I hope one of you has got a phone that does video. I'm not corrupting my nice straight phone with you arse-fucking."

"You can delete it after we've got a copy."

"I'm not fucking deleting it, because it won't be on my phone in the first place. My phone is proper homophobic. It'll refuse to film it. It'll just shut down as soon as it sees your dick going anywhere near his arse."

Dan's laughing, but I think he's serious about not using his phone. I really can't work him out sometimes.

Ryan looks across. "Mine's shit. It only films about a minute."

I'm just about to say the same thing when James comes to the rescue. "I've got a video camera. Only a little one, but it's okay. I've got quite a lot of electronic stuff, actually. You know, gadgets and things. All sorts."

Why am I not surprised? "James, you're a star. Fucking ace! When are we going to do this, then?"

Ryan's ready with an answer. "Well, I think it should be tomorrow. Don't want to leave Dan waiting too long, or he might get too excited." I look across to where Dan is standing, and he's got both middle fingers raised, one for each of us. Ryan carries on, a big smile on his face. "And it will give us time to recover a bit. You know, we've used up a lot of energy today—"

"And a lot of spunk."

"And a lot of spunk. So I think we need a night to recover." I see a new thought register on his face. "Actually, we could sleep together, couldn't we? I mean, if you want to. But not do anything, you know. Just spend the night together."

"That would be so cool."

James's voice again, "We can have, like, a gay room and a straight room. One for you two, and one for me and Dan. If you don't mind." He turns enquiringly toward Dan.

"No, of course I don't mind. I don't think it's going to be like the other day. Things are a bit fucking different, aren't they?"

James looks thoughtful. "Oh yes. I think so. Well, I hope so. Actually, this is how it was supposed to be all along."

I'm a bit confused. "What is?"

"You and Ryan sharing, and me and Dan sharing. That's how it started out."

I think back to the time when I arrived, with my mum and dad helping me carry my stuff into my room, and wondering who I'd be sharing with. Making my list of all the reasons I didn't want to share a room. Fucking hell, how quickly things can change.

It doesn't take long to sort things out. We're going to use this room for the filming tomorrow, but Dan and James are going to use it tonight. Ryan and I get dressed, ready to walk across to the other room. But by the time we're ready to go, Dan has another joint ready. "Bit of this, before you go?"

Chapter Ten

When I wake up, the sun's streaming in through the window. We must have forgotten to shut the curtains last night. I look across to my right, and there's Ryan lying next to me, still asleep.

My head doesn't feel too bad actually, despite the amount we smoked last night. I try to remember how many joints we had, but it's a bit of a blur, and I lose count after the third one. James smoked quite a lot, and was hilarious. Dan got louder and louder, and more and more rude, which was funny as well.

I don't remember much about getting back to the room and going to bed. I think we were both a bit too fucked to do anything except go to sleep straightaway. Anyway, we'd agreed to save ourselves for the filming today.

I turn on my side and push the duvet down so I can get a better look at Ryan. He's naked and his cock is rock hard. This is so cool. I move my hand down between my legs and give my hard-on a few tugs while I watch him sleep. This is the first time I've slept with a guy, and waking up and finding Ryan next to me is so exciting. I wonder why I haven't done this before. I started wanking when I was eleven, and spunked up the first time just before my twelfth birthday. I could have been having sex and having a boyfriend for years by now. I'm such a fucking idiot!

Still, at least it's happening now. There's plenty of time to make up for what I've missed out on so far.

The word "boyfriend" comes back into my head again. Shit, is that what Ryan is? A boyfriend? Well, I suppose he can't be a real boyfriend, not yet. We haven't talked about it at all, and we've only known each other for a couple of days. But it does feel a bit like being boyfriends, spending the night together. And today we're going to have proper sex. I hope I don't fuck it up. There's all kinds of things that can go wrong, aren't there? What if I can't get hard, or what if we can't get it to go in, or what if it hurts too much and we have to stop?

I'm just telling myself not to be so stupid when Ryan starts to wake up. He stretches and opens his eyes, and then smiles, and rolls over on top of me. The next thing I know, his tongue is pushing into my mouth, and he's grinding his cock against mine.

"Ryan, stop."

"What's the matter?"

"If you do that, you'll make me cum. We're supposed to be saving it, remember?"

Ryan looks up for a few moments, completely confused. Then it all comes back to him. "Oh, yeah. We're doing the filming today, aren't we? Shit, I forgot."

"Do you still want to?"

"Course I do. It's going to be so hot. Are you still all right with it?"

"Yeah! I can't wait."

"Cool."

Ryan settles back on top of me and kisses me again. I let my hands run over his back and down to his arse.

"Ryan. Do you think we'll manage it all right? I mean, I was just thinking. Loads of people say their first time was crap, don't they? I don't want to fuck it up."

Ryan takes his weight on his elbows and looks down at me. "It'll be awesome. Don't worry."

"What if I can't get it up? You know, stress. What do they call it? Performance something?"

I feel his hips move and his body grinds against my cock. "I don't think that's going to be a problem, do you?"

"Probably not." I can't help smiling at the thought of what's about to happen, and then suddenly we're kissing each other again.

I remember that there's one more thing I need to ask. I can't talk because Ryan's tongue is in my mouth, so I tap him a few times on the shoulder, and he stops kissing me and looks down. "What's the matter?"

"Nothing. It's fine. I was just thinking about condoms."

"What about them?"

"Will we need to use one? I mean, if we're both virgins, we won't need to, will we? But I wasn't sure what, well, you didn't tell me exactly what happened with that guy who attacked you."

"Oh, I see. No, it's okay. I was really worried after it happened, you know, so I ended up going to the clinic. I told the doctor exactly what the guy had done, and she said it was very unlikely I'd have caught anything, but I should have all the tests to make sure, and to set my mind at rest. So I did, and it's fine."

"Thank God for that."

"Yeah, I know. I was really panicking for a bit. I was imagining I'd caught HIV or something."

"Shit, I wasn't thinking of that! Yeah, thank God you didn't catch anything."

"What? What were you thinking about then?"

I wince. "Oh, fuck. Now I feel really bad."

"Come on. Out with it."

"Well, I was actually thinking, thank God I don't have to put a condom on, because I'm shit at it. I've only tried a couple of times, and it was a bit of a disaster both times. I couldn't get it on properly. And there wasn't even anyone else there, and no video camera."

"Are you telling me you were more worried about looking good on the video than about me catching AIDS off some psycho?" I cast a worried look up at Ryan, but he's smiling. Thank fuck for that.

"Sorry."

"It's okay. But I might have to beat you up anyway, you bastard."

With that, Ryan digs his fingers into my ribs and starts to tickle me mercilessly. I try to fight back, and the two of us are soon squirming about on the bed, laughing hysterically. Suddenly, I'm aware that I'm kind of upside-down, which doesn't seem right, and a moment later, we're both on the floor, with Ryan sprawled on top of me. The beds are quite low, fortunately, so there's no harm done.

"Shit, Tom. You all right?"

I put on a mock pained expression. "I think I might live. I've probably got a broken leg, and maybe a broken arm as well."

Ryan gives me a grin. "As long as you haven't broken your dick."

"And I expect I'll be covered in bruises by tomorrow."

"You poor thing."

"Well, if anyone asks, I'll have to tell them that my boyfriend beat me up." Oh my God, I didn't plan to say that! It just came out before I even thought about it. There's a short silence, while I look at Ryan and wait to see how he reacts.

He looks at me and opens and closes his mouth a couple of times before he actually speaks. "Did you say 'boyfriend' just then?"

"Um, I think I might have done. I don't quite remember—"

Ryan grabs me harder than ever, kissing me and squeezing me so tight I'm having trouble getting my breath. Looks like it was the right thing to say. Thank fuck for that. Eventually, he starts to loosen his grip a bit, and I get the chance to speak. "So is that okay with you, then?"

"What does it look like? Boyfriend. Fucking hell!" Ryan's got the biggest grin on his face, as he moves in for some more snogging. It's ages before we've had enough and are ready to get up.

"Shower before sex, or after?"

Ryan grins back at me. "Think it had better be after. If I go in the shower with you now, I won't be able to stop myself doing stuff to you. And we're saving it all for the camera, aren't we?"

"Yep. Every drop."

Ryan goes to the wardrobe and peers inside. "I can't wear jeans. All mine are dead skinny. I'll never get them done up when my dick's this hard." He starts sorting through his stuff. "I've got some trackies somewhere."

While Ryan finds something to wear, I put on the stuff that I dropped on the floor last night. I reach in and take some of Ryan's clean socks and then slip my feet into Dan's trainers again, and we're sorted.

As we're going downstairs, I hear Ryan muttering to himself, "Boyfriend…Boyfriend…This is my boyfriend…Hi, I'm Ryan, and this is my boyfriend…Hi, this is my boyfriend, Tom." He turns to face me, the huge grin still on his face, and he slides his hand into mine as we walk.

A couple of minutes later, we're outside my room, although I'm not sure if it is my room anymore. Looks like it's going to be Dan and James's room from now on.

James is up and not looking too bad, though he does say that he's feeling dizzy and a bit weird. If that's all he's feeling after last night, he's doing pretty well. He's wearing Dan's "Masturbating is not a Crime" T-shirt. It seems so ironic that I start laughing my ass off, but James is proper serious about it.

"I'm wearing it all day," he tells us, "I've already been down to the supermarket. Quite a few people noticed it; I could tell. A girl in the checkout queue looked at it and smiled. It made me get a bit hard."

"You dirty fucker." Ryan grins at him. "Have you always been this filthy, you know, inside?"

"I suppose I have. I just tried to pretend to myself I wasn't."

I turn to the bed, where Dan's lying with his hands behind his head and listening to the conversation. "You getting up then?"

"Why? There's no rush, is there?"

"Come on, Dan, don't fuck about. Get up now! We're ready for doing the filming."

"Okay, okay." I watch as Dan throws back the covers and starts to get up. I can tell Ryan's watching him too.

"So no boner this morning? That's a shame." I can't believe how much Ryan flirts with Dan.

"No, you cheeky fucker. Unlike some people"—he looks across at me—"I am able to show self-control and understand that there's a proper time and place for getting boned up."

James laughs. "He's just had a wank. He was finishing off when I got back from the shop."

Dan looks over at James. "You can shut the fuck up as well." But he's smiling as he says it.

"Wear your rugby shorts." It's Ryan again.

"What?"

"Wear your rugby shorts. For the filming. You look so hot in your rugby stuff."

"Fucking hell. All right, but keep your hands off me, okay?"

"Yeah, okay. I'll look but not touch. If that's what you want."

Dan goes to get dressed, and James brings the video camera across to show us. He tells us it's all charged and ready to go, and then goes over to Dan to show him how to do the zoom and one or two other things.

James is going into town, he tells us, to get some clothes and a haircut. Ryan offers to go with him later on, but James says he'd rather go straightaway. I don't know if he wants to get away from what's about to happen here, or if he really does want to handle the shopping trip by himself. One way or the other, he's soon ready, and he disappears to get the bus.

By this time, Dan's just finishing cleaning his teeth, and I think he's about ready too. I suppose this is it, then. I look over at Ryan, and he smiles back at me. Now it's actually happening, it doesn't feel quite how I was expecting. The whole thing seems a bit, well, awkward. I'm not sure what to do, how to get started. Perhaps this wasn't a good idea after all.

I wonder if Ryan's feeling the same. He goes over to James's computer desk where the camera is, picks it up, turns it over in his hands, and then switches it on. He hands it to Dan, who looks into the viewfinder and tries out the zoom.

I look across at Ryan again. I think I ought to tell him how awkward I'm feeling, but I'm not sure how to say it.

Too late. Before I can decide what to say, Ryan turns to Dan. "Come on, then. Point that thing at me, cause I'm ready to get started."

Dan swings the camera round, and the next thing I know Ryan launches himself at me, pushes me backward, and knocks me over onto the bed. I just have time to think that Ryan obviously isn't feeling the same as me, thank fuck, before his tongue pushes into my mouth and his hand goes down the front of my jeans. It takes about five seconds before

I forget all my worries and start getting into it. Ryan's hand starts getting me hard straightaway. I can tell he's still boned up. I can feel it pressing against me through his trackies. Fuck, what was I worrying about? This is going to be so fucking hot!

Ryan gets me properly hard in a few seconds, and then rolls off me, lying by my side and feeling over the front of my jeans. Suddenly, I hear him call out to Dan, "Get in closer; you're too far away."

Dan's concentrating on the camera. "You're all right, mate. I'll stay here. I can zoom in if you want."

"Fuck that. Get over here and film it properly." Dan hesitates, and Ryan turns to talk straight into the camera, a big grin on his face. "So, ladies and gentlemen, your cameraman for today's event is Dan, who says he's up for anything, but then fucking bottles out when things get serious. This is the guy who lost the soggy biscuit game last night, and then wouldn't eat it, even though—"

"All right. Shut the fuck up. I'm coming closer, okay?" He moves forward, keeping his eye on the viewfinder screen.

Ryan watches him. "On your knees, straight boy. You'll get a much better view if you're down lower."

Dan lowers the camera for a moment and looks at us. "You are a pair of complete cunts, you know that? I wish I'd never met either of you. I mean that." But there's something in his face that makes it obvious he doesn't mean it at all.

Ryan laughs. "Okay, okay. But it's too late for that, so shut the fuck up and get filming. It's time to see a bit of cock, yeah?"

I'm definitely up for that. I get a massive buzz of excitement thinking about the whole thing. All my nerves have gone. Ryan's lying next to me, the camera's on me, and Dan's kneeling right in front of me with his knees way apart and his rugby shorts stretched tight across his crotch. Fucking hell. Ryan's hand moves across the front of my jeans again and undoes the buttons. He rubs his hand over my boxers, and I can see the shape of my nob clearly through the material. He traces his finger slowly up and down the shaft of my cock, and a little dark patch appears on my boxers. Ryan rubs it with his finger. "Mmm, horny boy."

He pulls my jeans off and then puts his hand on my thigh and moves it up, slipping his fingers inside my boxers and up to my ball sack. He squeezes. Not hard, but hard enough to make me tense up and grunt. Then his hand carries on moving upward and closes round my cock. I can see the exact shape of Ryan's hand and the top of my cock stretched tight against the thin material of my boxers, and the stain of the pre-cum spreading.

After wanking me gently for a few seconds, he brings his hand out and takes hold of the waistband, pulling my boxers down and releasing my cock. It twitches and jumps around like it's got a life of its own, but I suppose it has. He leans over me and brings his head down to take my bell-end in his mouth. I feel his tongue rub across the really sensitive bit on the end of my nob, and his hand squeezes the shaft quite hard. Immediately, I feel my muscles start to tighten like I'm going to cum. I grab his head and pull it away. "Fuck, Ryan, if you do that I'm going to cum, like, now!"

His eyes turn toward me. "Want me to slow down?"

"I think you're going to have to. I don't know how I'm going to hold this back."

"Think about something that's not sexy. That's what they say, isn't it?"

"Fuck that!" It's Dan. I'd almost forgotten that he was still there. "You're supposed to be making a porno. Why would you want to think about stuff that's not sexy? Just make him cum, Ryan. He'll be hard again in about two seconds. I've seen what this animal's like. He might last a bit longer after he's cum once, you know; be a better fuck for both of you if he lasts longer."

Ryan looks back at me. "What do you think?"

"He's probably right. I'm so horny I don't think I'll be able to stop myself cumming anyway."

"Cool. Let's do it." He turns his head toward Dan. "Right. I want this load in my mouth. Bring the camera right up close. Don't miss any of it."

Ryan kneels up, as if he's thinking about how to do this, and then clambers over me and lies down on his back on the edge of the bed, near to where Dan is with the camera. "Turn on your side."

I do as he says, moving up the bed so my cock is level with his face. It's a bit of an awkward position, and Ryan's not happy with it. "Get a pillow. Put it under you." I reach up, grab the pillow, and shove it under my hips. My cock's a bit higher up now, sort of level with Ryan's face. Ryan grins at me and then says to Dan, "Okay get the camera right in here!"

I hear Dan muttering, "Fuck's sake," but next thing he's kneeling on the bed, straddling Ryan, and pointing the camera down at us. I swear he's got a hard-on. At least if he hasn't, his shorts have gone a weird shape. Fucking hell, I'm so turned on it's untrue.

Ryan turns his head back toward me. "Right, you'd better aim this well. I want all this load straight down my throat. Okay, dirty boy?"

"Ryan, you do it."

"What?"

"You wank me. It'll be super-hot if you do it. And you can point it where you want it."

"Fuck, yeah. Tell me when you're going to shoot it."

"Okay."

Ryan's hand comes round and takes hold of my cock. He starts really slowly and gradually speeds up. It's not going to take long. I stretch my body out and then look down Ryan's body, his trackies tented up with his hard-on, and Dan kneeling over him. I bend my leg and push my foot in through the small triangle between Ryan's crotch and Dan's legs. I feel the shape of Ryan's cock pressing on one side of my leg and Dan's leg hair rubbing on the other. Fuck! That's all I need to get me cumming instantly.

"Oh God. Cum!" is all I can manage to shout before my body tenses up and starts shooting. I'm trying to keep kind of still so the cum goes in Ryan's mouth, but the feeling's so intense, it's really difficult. I can see the squirts of cum shooting, but it's hard to see exactly where they're going.

Eventually, the orgasm starts to fade, and Ryan's hand slows down and then stops. I push myself up on one elbow and look down at Ryan. He's pretty well covered with it. "Shit, Ryan. Did you miss your mouth? It's all gone on your face."

"No. Loads of it went in my mouth. You shot bucket loads of the stuff. You nearly fucking drowned me."

"Cool. Well, that shows how hot it was! Fucking hell. Right, do you want me to clean you up? Are there some tissues somewhere?"

Before he can answer, Dan's voice cuts in, "What are you talking about? Don't you two know anything about gay sex? Bit of cum play, guys, for the camera, you know?"

I'm a bit lost. "What?"

"Fuck's sake. I feel like I know more about this than you do. Just get down there and lick it off. Then you—Oh fucking hell, what am I saying? I shouldn't have to tell you what to do. Fucking make something up. Shit!"

Ryan grins at me, with a trail of cum starting to run down one cheek. "Yeah, Tom, fucking make something up. Come on, then."

I don't need any more ideas. I'm already sliding down the bed to get to Ryan. My leg slips further in between Dan's legs, and for a moment, it rubs against his crotch. I'm pretty sure I can feel something proper hard in there, but he immediately kneels up higher, so his cock is out of reach of my leg, and I can't be absolutely certain.

Ryan turns the spunky side of his face toward me and grins. He's turning into such a little cum-slut I can't believe it. I remember the night before, Ryan licking cum off James's hand after the circle jerk. I take hold of his head and tilt it so I can get to work cleaning him up. The big grin never leaves his face as I work my tongue over him, cleaning off as much of the gooey mess as I can.

Ryan puts a hand on my shoulder. "Don't swallow it yet." He turns his head back and locks his mouth on mine, pushing inside with his tongue. It feels kind of weird, feeling my juice going back and forth between us as we kiss. At first, I'm not one hundred percent sure whether I like it or not, but Ryan's really into it, and it doesn't take long to win me over.

In the end, we both fall back onto the bed and look down at ourselves and at Dan, kneeling over our legs. Ryan's cock is making a very big bulge in his trackies, and I reach in and give it a feel. It's still very hard.

Mine's still quite hard too. Looks like it isn't going to go down. Brilliant. That means I'll be able to get started on Ryan's arse more or less straightaway.

I look at Ryan and follow his gaze. He's looking at Dan's shorts. "Dan, you've got a boner, haven't you?"

"Have I fuck!"

"You have. I can tell. I can see the shape of it in your shorts."

"Fuck off. I have not got a boner. Why the fuck would I get a boner over you two?"

"I don't know, but you've got one anyway."

"That's bollocks."

"Prove it."

"Fuck off."

"Prove it! Pull your shorts down and then we'll know."

"I'm not pulling my shorts down so you two benders can perv at my nob *again*."

I look at Ryan. "You must be right, then. He'd show us otherwise. I thought he was boned up, I noticed a bit ago, but I wasn't quite sure."

Dan's voice is starting to get louder. "You two are so full of shit. I haven't got a boner. I may have, well, a little bit of a semi, but that's all. And that's only because you're, you know, you're having sex, and sex is—"

"Sexy?" Ryan suggests.

"Yeah. Sex is a turn-on. Even if it's two blokes, it's still a bit of a turn-on."

"Fair enough. That's cool." Ryan nods and raises his eyebrows in my direction.

Dan goes on, "And anyway, I didn't have a wank this morning, and I always get hard easily when I haven't had a wank."

This time it's my turn to chip in. "James said you did have a wank this morning."

"What? Oh, er, well, I did have *one* wank, yes, that's true, but it was only a little one, and it was ages ago."

Ryan and I catch each other's eye and both crack up. A few seconds later, Dan's smiling too. Ryan lifts his leg and puts his foot right onto Dan's crotch. "Let's see what a bit of a semi feels like, shall we?"

Dan grabs his leg and pushes it away, but not before Ryan's scientific research has paid off. "Fucking hell, Dan. You call that a semi? It felt like a fucking metal bar in there."

Dan opens and closes his mouth before he thinks of a reply. "Well, yeah, it's quite hard *now*. That's because you made me think about having a wank, and that made it go hard. It was only a semi till then."

"Whatever." Ryan doesn't sound convinced, and he's laughing again. "I just wish all straight boys got hard like that watching gay sex."

"Fuck off. Anyway, are we going to talk about my dick all day, or are you two going to fuck?"

"We're going to fuck," Ryan says, "but I thought we might have to wait a bit for Tom to get hard again."

All three of us look at my dick. It's really solid. Ryan reaches over and gives it a feel. "Well, looks like I was wrong about that, then. Let's do this. I'm so fucking excited! Have you got the lube?"

I untangle myself from Ryan and Dan and slide off the bed. Someone's put my bag away in the cupboard—James I expect—and it takes me a while to find it. The lube is down at the bottom of the bag, under some porn DVDs. When I turn round to go back to the bed, Ryan's got both legs in the air, and a finger shoved right inside his arse. Dan's filming him as he slides his finger in and out.

"Fucking hell, Ryan, I didn't say you could start without me."

"Just getting my hole warmed up."

Dan lets the camera drop a bit and looks at both of us in turn. "What he's going to stick in you is a bit bigger than a finger, you know. Hope you're ready for it."

Ryan doesn't look a bit worried. "It's fine. I've had plenty of practice with my toys."

I think this actually surprises Dan. "Toys? I thought you were an innocent little boy till Tom got hold of you."

"You must be joking! He's the innocent one. I've been sticking stuff up here since I was about fifteen. Then, when I hit eighteen, I got some proper toys. Want me to tell you all about them?"

"Shit, no! Fucking hell." Dan shakes his head a couple of times and returns his attention to the camera.

I turn back to Ryan. He's looking super-hot, lying there staring at me, his eyes shining, and just slowly moving his finger in and out of his hole. Fuck, it's such a turn-on, seeing him doing that. I feel my nob pulse and jolt, and looking down, there's some pre-cum oozing out.

"Right, you," Ryan says, "Get over here!" I'm there in about two seconds. I kind of fall on top of him, kissing him and running my hands up and down his body. But he's too excited to want that to go on for long. He rolls us over, so he can sit on my legs, and takes the lube off me. He squeezes a big dollop of it onto his hand and grabs my cock, massaging it in. Then he gets some more out of the tube and reaches between his legs.

"Ryan, how are we going to do this? I mean, what position are we going to try?"

"Oh, don't worry about that. I've got everything sorted out."

"What do you mean, you've got everything sorted out?"

"It's all planned. I know exactly what I want us to do. I've been imagining this for so long. You just let me take control, yeah, like you did the other day. You all right with that?"

"Fucking hell, yeah. Just tell me what to do."

"Okay. Right. Well, I'm going on my side, like this, and you're going behind me." He gets us arranged on the bed, with me kind of snuggled up behind him, and then he lifts his leg right up and holds it there with his hand. "Now, Dan comes in close with the camera, and you get your nob lined up and stick it in. No probs." He turns his head and grins at me.

"But I can't see your arse from here."

Dan looks out from behind the camera. "Well, fucking move then, you retard."

"Oh, yeah, I suppose." I twist round on the bed and lift my head up to where I can get a view of Ryan's arse, the hole all sticky with lube, and guide my bell-end toward it. "Do you want me to go slow, in case it hurts too much?"

"No. Just fucking do it. It'll be fine, I've told you."

"You sure?"

"I'm sure."

I wriggle forward a bit and push my bell-end against Ryan's hole, which opens up straightaway. I take hold of his shoulders and pull myself up, feeling the whole length of my nob sliding inside. Ryan tenses up and takes a deep breath, but then relaxes again.

"Okay?"

"Yeah, more than okay. Now fuck me."

I start to move my hips and feel the excitement rising in me immediately. I can't believe I'm actually doing this at last! I keep one of my hands hooked over Ryan's shoulder and move the other one over his body, so I can take hold of his cock and wank it.

Ryan lets out a moan, "Yeah, keep doing that. Fuck harder if you want."

I hear Dan's voice from behind the camera. "Shit, you must have been doing a lot of practicing. Doesn't that hurt like fuck? Look at the size of that thing going in there."

Ryan's starting to breathe hard already as he replies, "Yeah, it hurts. It's fucking amazing. Do it more. Do it harder!"

I try to do as I'm told, speeding up and trying to control it so my nob doesn't slip out, and I start to get a good rhythm going. After a bit, I feel myself getting close to cumming, and have to slow down. I move really slowly for a bit, just concentrating on wanking Ryan and kissing the back of his neck.

Then I feel his hand running through my hair. "Okay, I'm going to turn over now. Slide it out for a bit." He pulls away from me, and my cock slides out, still hard and glistening with lube. Ryan turns over on his back, and I wait to be told what to do. But he speaks to Dan first. "Okay Dan, you come round here." He points to the top of the bed. "Kneel up on the bed and get your knees on either side of my head." Dan doesn't object and starts to move into position. "That's it."

Dan's kneeling with Ryan's head virtually in his crotch, and his legs wide open on either side of Ryan's shoulders. He looks fucking hot. His shorts are stretched tight, and his boner is really obvious now. He sees me looking but just turns his attention back to the camera and doesn't even try to disguise it.

Ryan lifts his legs in the air, grabbing an ankle with each hand, but then lets them down again. "I nearly forgot. Little extra present for you, Tom. Dan, pass me your trainers."

"What?"

"Your trainers. Take them off and pass them here."

Dan does as he's told without making a fuss, although I can hear him muttering, "Fucking hell, not again."

Ryan slips the trainers onto his own feet and looks at me. "These the ones you spunked on?"

"Yeah."

"Dirty boy. You ready to fuck me?" He takes hold of his ankles again, and this time he lifts his legs right up in the air and keeps them there. "Grab a pillow and stick it under me." I reach for one, and maneuver it under Ryan's arse. I move into position, kneeling and shuffling forward, taking hold of Ryan's legs to help me get into exactly the right place. I reach for the lube, squeeze a bit more onto Ryan's hole, and then slide forward. This time I get a full view of my cock sliding inside, and it's so fucking hot watching it. Ryan lets out a gasp and then moves his legs so that his feet are resting on my shoulders. Dan's trainers are on either side of my head, and I get a faint smell of sweat from them. Even more fucking hot!

I start moving and try to work out what to do. It's a bit more awkward to get the hang of it, kneeling like this, but I soon find that if I lean forward a bit and put my hands on the bed on either side of Ryan's waist, it all starts working amazingly. I'm so turned on that I soon have to slow down again to stop myself cumming, and that gives me a chance to do some serious wanking on Ryan's cock.

"How's that feeling?"

"Fucking brilliant." Suddenly, Ryan's hand goes up over his head and drops onto Dan's leg, where it starts to move up inside his rugby shorts. Fucking hell, is Dan going to let him get away with that? I look up at Dan, but he seems to be concentrating on the filming. I can see Ryan's hand moving inside Dan's shorts, and Dan's letting him do it. "Fucking hell, it's soaking wet in here. There's so much pre-cum." I wait for Dan to say something, but he doesn't. "Dan, I can't get it out. These shorts are too tight. Help me."

One of Dan's hands lets go of the camera and pulls at the bottom of his shorts, moving them away from his leg and giving Ryan enough room to get his nob out. It's completely hard and just as beautiful as I remembered it. There's a strand of pre-cum stretching right across from the hairs on Dan's thigh to his bell-end. Jesus Christ! I think if I move at all, I'm going to shoot my load.

Ryan grabs hold of Dan's cock and starts wanking it. Dan's breathing changes straightaway. He must be really turned on despite all that bullshit about only having a "bit of a semi." I think he's going to cum really quickly.

Ryan obviously thinks so too. "Right, Tom, get your mouth round this fucker. There's another present on the way." My eyes flick up to Dan's face, but all his attention's on the camera. I'm not sure I dare do this. I'm remembering all that stuff about not touching Dan.

Ryan cuts in, "Dan, where's the camera pointing? You getting this?"

"What? Oh yeah." I see the camera swivel downward, and Ryan's hand starts to speed up a bit, wanking Dan quite fast now. Dan kneels up, his chest rising and falling with his breathing. Oh, fuck it, I'm just going to do it. What's the worst that can happen? I lean forward a bit further, so that my mouth is right next to Dan's shiny, wet bell-end. I reach out with my hand and grab his ball sack, and then open my mouth. I'm only just in time. He lets out a big grunt, and starts cumming almost at once. I feel the first shot hitting the roof of my mouth, then one going right to the back of my tongue. My mouth closes instinctively. I can't stop it happening, and the next big wet splodge hits me right in the face. I manage to get my mouth open again in time for the last bits to squeeze out onto my tongue, and immediately, Ryan pulls me down on top of him and presses his mouth onto mine. Because I'm lying on top of Ryan, all Dan's cum dribbles straight down out of my mouth into Ryan's. He's loving it, running his tongue over my lips, and I can feel him tightening and relaxing his arse muscles around my cock.

Then I feel Ryan's hands on either side of my head, pulling our mouths apart. "Tom, I need to cum. Make me cum!"

This is going to be good. Fuck, this is going to be so good. I kneel up again and have a good, long look at Ryan. His head is right between Dan's legs. Dan's cock is beginning to droop a bit and is just above Ryan's forehead. His body is stretched out under me; he looks so skinny, and so hot. His legs are still in the air, with my cock disappearing into the hole in between them. His cock is jerking around on its own as I reach out and take hold.

"Okay, here we go."

I start to move my hips back and forth a bit, getting my nob moving in and out of Ryan's hole again. I'm just about to start wanking him when I remember the lube. I'm sure He'll enjoy it more if he's lubed up. I have a quick look round the bed, but I can't see the tube anywhere, and I'm not stopping to go and search for it. Fuck it. I have another idea, and position my head over Ryan's cock. My mouth's still really wet from Dan's cum and Ryan's saliva, and it's easy to make a big mouthful of sticky wetness, which I start to dribble down onto Ryan's tight red bell-end.

I get my hand moving now and massage the liquid in a bit, trying to keep some slow fucking going at the same time. Ryan's watching me wanking him, as I speed up my hand and fuck a bit harder. He's making loads of noise now, which is a fucking big turn-on for me, too, and he grabs at my knees with both hands.

I start to feel him tensing up. I know what that means, and he doesn't need to tell me he's cumming. His eyes lock onto mine, his fingers dig into my legs, and his spunk starts shooting out onto his chest. He shouts out with each spurt, and his body shudders. Fuck, it's all so hot!

He hasn't even finished cumming when he grabs my hand, takes it off his cock, and says, "Right, Tom. Cum in me now. Fuck me hard and cum in me."

"But, Ryan, what about the video? Don't you want a cum-shot for the video?"

"Fuck that! I don't care. I want you to shoot it inside me." With that, his feet are up on my shoulders again, and I feel Dan's trainers rubbing against the side of my head. Ryan grabs a handful of the sheet and grips it tight. "Fucking do it."

I let myself drop forward onto Ryan, and hear him gasp as my cock pushes deep inside him. I get my hands kind of hooked under his shoulders and start fucking. I know I'm only going to last a few seconds before I cum, and I'm determined that it's going to be something Ryan will remember for a long time. I can't build up slowly or anything like that. I'm too excited. I just have to start thrusting like some mad fucker straightaway.

Ryan's grunting and shouting out, "Yeah! Yeah!" and grabbing at the bedsheets. Every thrust sends his head further back into Dan's crotch.

The orgasm starts slowly, like it's coming at me from a long way away, but it builds and builds, and after a few seconds, it's taking me over. I want to say something. I want to tell Ryan how amazing this is, and how it's the most incredible feeling ever, but I can't speak. All I can do is fuck and fuck and fuck, feeling the spunk shooting and shooting, and then dribbling and then finally stopping.

I let myself down from my elbows to lie on top of Ryan. I am absolutely fucking exhausted and still can't speak. Ryan takes hold of me, wrapping his arms round my back and stroking my skin as I start to get my breath back and come down from the orgasm.

Above me, I hear a click as Dan switches off the camera. "Well, you're going to have to edit this shit yourselves, because I'm not fucking doing it."

EPILOGUE

It's Saturday evening and we're all set to go out. It's the end of term, so everyone's going home over the next few days, and this is our last chance to all be together for a few weeks.

I'm spending quite a lot of the holiday at Ryan's. He's told his mum everything that's been going on, and it seems like she's fine with it all. By the sound of it, she wasn't that surprised by Ryan telling her he was gay, or that he had a boyfriend. She said she'd kind of guessed, apparently. I've spoken to her on the phone a couple of times, and she sounds great. I don't think it's going to be too awkward; maybe a bit at first, but not for long.

The conversation with my parents *is* going to be awkward. I haven't told them anything yet. My mum rings me quite a lot, but I just keep the conversations sort of general and try to keep off dodgy subjects altogether. I'm not looking forward to it at all, but it's something I've got to get through. Thank God, I'm not going to be home for too long before I go to Ryan's. It will give them a chance to get over it.

The plan for tonight is: pub first, then pizza, then a bar, and then a club.

We're meeting James and Katie at the pub. They'll be on time, so we had better get moving soon. James and Katie have been an item for ages now. It sounds like it's going pretty well so far. James tells us everything that they get up to, all the horny details. I bet Katie doesn't know he tells his mates all about their sex life, but what the fuck?

Dan's got a new girlfriend, who we haven't met yet. This is his third girlfriend since September. I hope this one lasts a bit longer than the others. They're meeting us at some point as well, but Dan's always late for everything, so we won't wait for them.

I turn round from the mirror, where I've been sorting out my hair, and look at Ryan, who's lying on the bed, with his hands behind his head, watching me. "Are you looking at my arse, you fucking pervert?"

"Just thinking how hot you look."

"You too, babe." He's in his skinny jeans and Converse, and looking fit as fuck. "Suppose we should get going."

"Suppose so." He moves up onto his elbows and gives me a smile. "Time for a quickie before we go?"

About the Author

Kev was born in Oxford, England, but not in one of the posh bits! He now lives and works in Africa, where he is easily recognizable as the tattooed white guy who cycles everywhere. As well as being a writer, he is a teacher, actor, and theater director. In 2010, he won the Guardian Newspaper's New Writers from Minority Backgrounds competition. He has written articles for the *Guardian*, short stories, and two full-length plays.

Straight Boy Roommate is his first novel.

Contact him at kevtrainerboy@gmail.com.

Books Available from Bold Strokes Books

Tricks of the Trade: Magical Gay Erotica edited by Jerry L. Wheeler. Today's hottest erotica writers take you inside the sultry, seductive world of magicians and their tricks-professional and otherwise. (978-1-60282-781-3)

Straight Boy Roommate by Kev Troughton. Tom isn't expecting much from his first term at University, but a chance encounter with straight boy Dan catapults him into an extraordinary, wild weekend of sex and self-discovery, which turns his life upside down, and leads him into his first love affair. (978-1-60282-782-0)

The Jesus Injection by Eric Andrews-Katz. Murderous statues, demented drag queens, political bombings, ex-gay ministries, espionage, and romance are all in a day's work for a top-secret agent. But the gloves are off when Agent Buck 98 comes up against The Jesus Injection. (978-1-60282-762-2)

Combustion by Daniel W. Kelly. Bearish detective Deck Waxer comes to the city of Kremfort Cove to investigate why the hottest men in town are bursting into flames in broad daylight. (978-1-60282-763-9)

Raising Hell: Demonic Gay Erotica edited by Todd Gregory. *Raising Hell*: hot stories of gay erotica featuring demons. (978-1-60282-768-4)

Pursued by Joel Gomez-Dossi. Openly gay college student Jamie Bradford becomes romantically involved with two men at the same time, and his hell begins when one of his boyfriends becomes intent on killing him. (978-1-60282-769-1)

Young Bucks: Novellas of Twenty-Something Lust & Love edited by Richard Labonte. Four writers still in their twenties—or with their twenties a nearby memory—write about what it's like to be young, on the prowl for sex, or looking to fall in love. (978-1-60282-770-7)

Night Shadows: Queer Horror edited by Greg Herren and J.M. Redmann. *Night Shadows* features delightfully wicked stories by some of the biggest names in queer publishing. (978-1-60282-751-6)

Secret Societies by William Holden. An outcast hustler, his unlikely "mother," his faithless lovers, and his religious persecutors—all in 1726. (978-1-60282-752-3)

Wyatt: Doc Holliday's Account of an Intimate Friendship by Dale Chase. Erotica writer Dale Chase takes the remarkable friendship between Wyatt Earp, upright lawman, and Doc Holliday, Southern gentlemen turned gambler and killer, to an entirely new level: hot! (978-1-60282-755-4)

The Jetsetters by David-Matthew Barnes. As rock band the Jetsetters skyrockets from obscurity to superstardom, Justin Holt, a lonely barista, and Diego Delgado, the band's guitarist, fight with everything they have to stay together, despite the chaos and fame. (978-1-60282-745-5)

Strange Bedfellows by Rob Byrnes. Partners in life and crime, Grant Lambert and Chase LaMarca are hired to make a politician's compromising photo disappear, but what should be an easy job quickly spins out of control. (978-1-60282-746-2)

Sweat: Gay Jock Erotica edited by Todd Gregory. Sizzling tales of smoking-hot sex with the athletic studs everyone fantasizes about. (978-1-60282-669-4)

The Marrying Kind by Ken O'Neill. Just when successful wedding planner Adam More decides to protest inequality by quitting the business and boycotting marriage entirely, his only sibling announces her engagement. (978-1-60282-670-0)

Boys of Summer edited by Steve Berman. Stories of young love and adventure, when the sky's ceiling is a bright blue marvel, when another boy's laughter at the beach can distract from dull summer jobs. (978-1-60282-663-2)

Calendar Boys by Logan Zachary. A man a month will keep you excited year round. (978-1-60282-665-6)

Buccaneer Island by J.P. Beausejour. In the rough world of Caribbean piracy, a man is what he makes of himself—or what a stronger man makes of him. (978-1-60282-658-8)

Twelve O'Clock Tales by Felice Picano. The fourth collection of short fiction by legendary novelist and memoirist Felice Picano. Thirteen dark tales that will thrill and disturb, discomfort and titillate, enthrall and leave you wondering. (978-1-60282-659-5)

Words to Die By by William Holden. Sixteen answers to the question: What causes a mind to curdle? (978-1-60282-653-3)